Niki Lenz

A Yearling Book

 Published in the United States by Yearling, an imprint of Random House Children's Books, a division of Penguin Random House LLC, New York. Originally published in hardcover in the United States by Random House Children's Books, a division of Penguin Random House LLC, New York, in 2019.

Visit us on the Web! rhcbooks.com

Educators and librarians, for a variety of teaching tools, visit us at RHTeachersLibrarians.com

The Library of Congress has cataloged the hardcover edition of this work as follows:
Name: Lenz, Niki, author.
Title: Bernice Buttman, model citizen / Niki Lenz.
Description: First edition. | New York: Random House, [2019] |
Summary: "Bernice Buttman is tired of being labeled a bully, so when her mom leaves her with her aunt, who is a nun, Bernice decides to mend her ways and become a model citizen"—Provided by publisher.
Identifiers: LCCN 2018039636 | ISBN 978-1-5247-7041-9 (hardcover) |
ISBN 978-1-5247-7044-0 (hardcover library binding) |
ISBN 978-1-5247-7042-6 (ebook)
Subjects: | CYAC: Conduct of life—Fiction. | Bullying—Fiction. | Nuns—Fiction. |
Aunts—Fiction. | Moving, Household—Fiction. | Humorous stories.
Classification: LCC PZ7.1.L45 Ber 2019 | DDC [Fic]—dc23

ISBN 978-1-5247-7043-3 (paperback)

Printed in the United States of America
10 9 8 7 6 5 4 3 2 1
First Yearling Edition 2021

To my mom, Sherry Brummett,
who taught me to read and took me to the library.
And to my dad, Richard Brummett,
who taught me to chase big, scary dreams.

Contents

Bernice Buttman, Model Citizen

1

Don't Go Breakin' My Heart

Here are things that I, Bernice Buttman, was awesome at. One: burping the alphabet. Two: blowing up stuff with firecrackers. Three: wearing the teachers and puny kids of Oak Grove Elementary School into nubs. I was less great at knowing what to do with myself at recess.

I sat on top of the monkey bars, feeling like a booger on a cheese ball . . . out of place and unwelcome. Kids whirled all around me, talking to their buddies and playing games, but nobody came within arm's length of me. That was probably real smart. There was only one kid in this whole mess who I didn't want to clobber.

Oliver Stratts stood in a small knot of kids, huddled against the wind. I stared at the back of his curly head while I swung my legs back and forth. Even though Oliver avoided me so he wouldn't get pounded like the rest of the kids, I had decided I wanted him to be my friend. He was real smart and he always smelled like name-brand laundry detergent and I'd never heard him answer a question wrong. I hoped he could be the first kid to play tag with me at recess and live to tell the tale. But how in blue blazes are you supposed to get someone to like you, anyhow?

"Bernice!" My momma's voice cut across the playground, making my heart yank into my throat. *What is she doing here?*

Momma leaned against the chain link fence, her face pressing through the metal diamonds. "Bernice Buttman, get your raggedy behind over here right this minute!"

I felt my face go pink as heads turned to see what the commotion was about. I half fell, half flipped off the top of the monkey bars and jogged past the gawkers, one hand yanking my pants up, my other arm wiping my nose with my sleeve.

"What are you doing here?" I hissed as soon as I was close enough to the fence. Momma was wearing pajama pants and slippers, even though it was eleven o'clock.

"Imma need my money back," she said, digging around in her purse for something.

"What money?" I scowled.

"The money I gave you this morning for your lunch," she said, as though this made perfect sense.

"But I need that money to eat!" I said, very aware of all the kids who were staring and pointing and laughing at that very second.

Momma threw her hands in the air as though I was being completely unreasonable. "I don't know, girl! You'll figure something out. Now cough up the cash. I gotta put gas in the car and get to my tattoo appointment."

Momma was getting me and my four older brothers' faces tattooed on her back. That was a whole lot of ugly, let me tell ya. Plus, it was so expensive she was having to shake down her daughter for lunch money.

I pushed the two dollar bills through the wires of the fence, just so she'd hurry up and get out of there. She stuffed the money in her pocket and waved, climbing into her clunker and exiting in a puff of smoke.

I stood there, clinging to the fence, taking deep breaths and trying to calm down. If I turned around and saw just one of those booger-eaters staring, they would be sorry.

Sometimes I missed when I was little and all us Buttmans were here at the elementary school together. If anyone messed with me, my big brothers would pound the pudding out of them. Kids learned right from the get-go to leave me alone. And I liked it that way.

Mostly.

Except for at recess when your mom shows up and steals your cash and is totally embarrassing and you wish you had a friend who would share his lunch with you.

It was time to put my plan in action.

I pulled the note out of my pocket and smoothed it on

my leg. My first version had been scrawled in marker, but I reckoned my handwriting looked too messy, so I'd redone it with letters cut out of a magazine.

DEAR OLIVER,
DO YOU WANT TO BE MY FRIEND?
YES OR NO
BERNICE

I'd wanted it to look fancy, but I think it might have ended up looking like a ransom note. I stared at the back of Oliver's head again and tried to decide if now was the right time to give him the note.

Gina Sullivan laughed her fool head off about something Oliver had said. I took a few steps closer, real stealthy-like, and strained to hear what they were saying.

"Did you see how many chins that woman had?" Gina said, loud enough that everyone within half a mile of the school could hear. My stomach suddenly felt cold as ice.

That loudmouth girl kept talking. "I'll betcha Bernice will look just like her when she's grown."

My hands balled up into fists.

Oliver's voice was quieter, but I still heard him plain as day. "I heard they steal toilet paper from the gas station bathroom."

Not him! The rest of the kids could talk, but not my soon-to-be best friend! My ears filled up with a roaring, and before I had a second to think things through, my feet had marched me right over to the group of snot-nosed fifth graders. The kids went quiet, and Oliver was suddenly very interested in the zipper on his jacket.

I grabbed one of his skinny arms and twisted it behind his back. The rest of the kids scattered like roaches in the sunlight.

"Ouch!" Oliver squealed.

"Come with me," I said, my voice as sweet as sunshine. "I've got a present for you."

"I don't want a present," Oliver said, his voice high and wobbly.

"Okay, then maybe *you've* got a present for *me*." I found the pile of dog doo I'd spotted earlier, and I pushed Oliver's face right up next to it. "There's something I've been meaning to ask you, Oliver. How would you feel about me and you being friends?"

"No way!" He tried to squirm out from under me, but I outweighed him by about a million pounds. All I had to do was lean forward a smidge, and his nose would touch poo. It would serve him right for talking bad about me in front of everyone, him being my best friend and all.

The little twerp's voice squeaked, and he talked through gritted teeth. "Oh, gosh! Oh, man. Let me up, Bernice!"

"I'll be glad to. When you say you'll be my friend."

"Okay, okay, fine," Oliver whined.

The recess bell rang and the other kids, who had been

watching us from a safe distance, ran to the redbrick wall to line up. I stood slowly and gave Oliver's backside one tiny kick, sending him sprawling only one beard-second away from the pile of dookie. (A beard-second is the average length a beard grows in one second. Google it.) He scrambled backward, pinching his nose. "You need Jesus, Buttman! You're the meanest girl I know!"

Maybe I did need Jesus, but at least my stomach wasn't gonna be grumbling at lunchtime. "Too bad for you, 'cause I'm your new best friend." I wadded up my friendship invitation and threw it at Oliver's head. "What did your mom pack me for lunch?"

2

Sunday School Bully

Everyone knew Oliver Stratts attended the First Baptist Church with his parents and older sister. He had cleaner fingernails than any person I'd ever met. I thought about those clean fingernails as I reached into the tub of cheese balls for breakfast that Sunday.

I wondered if Oliver would be surprised to see me if I showed up at church.

I wondered if my momma would even notice I'd left.

I wondered if they served snacks at Sunday school.

When I'd clawed the last ball out of the plastic jar and licked all the glow-in-the-dark orange powder off my fingers, I decided it was time I got religion.

The First Baptist Church was a short bike ride away from the Lone Star Trailer Park. I hocked a loogie at the sign as I pedaled past. The plastic letters N, E, T, and A had fallen to their deaths last winter, making the sign read

LO SR TRAILER PARK. Or Loser Trailer Park, as the kids at my school liked to call it. Just not to me, or they'd be sorry.

I was out of breath by the time I threw my bike on the steps of the church. The squat white building stood quiet and holy, and I hesitated with my hands on the heavy wooden doors. Sweat made little wading pools under my pits, and I started to smell ripe.

If you entered a church with the intent to mess with one of the patrons, would God be mad at you? And how mad are we talking? Like, you better do one good deed to make up for it, or a whole pile?

Who was I kidding? I wasn't gonna do any good deeds.

I barreled through the door and let the air conditioning blow the fuzzy yellow hair off my forehead like I'd stuck my finger in a light socket.

The big room full of wood pews was empty except for some old ladies practicing for the choir. They happily ushered a sinner to Sunday school, which it turned out was located in the damp church basement.

You should've seen Oliver's face.

He couldn't have been more surprised if the Little Lord Baby Jesus had walked through the door in his swaddling clothes.

And lucky me, the only empty folding chair in the circle of fifth graders sat right next to him. He tried to put his Bible there, but the Sunday school teacher pried it from his hands and placed it underneath. She smiled with super-white teeth. "Please, take a seat."

The chair squealed like a stuck pig when I sat down, and the other kids snickered. That didn't seem very Christian of them, but I wouldn't know Christian from nothin'. I smiled over at Oliver, my eyelashes fluttering like Miss Missouri's, and his face turned green as a grasshopper.

"Now, let's get back to our lesson," the skinny teacher lady said.

I raised my hand.

"Yes? Bernice, isn't it?" Her face glowed with excitement. It seemed my bad reputation had followed me to God's house. She must have thought I was gonna repent of my evil ways right then and there.

"You got snacks?" I asked. More snickering, but the kids were careful this time to cover their mouths. It mighta crossed their minds that I wasn't above punching someone in a church basement.

"Um, no," the teacher said, scrunching her brows. "But there will be Communion during the main service."

Unless they ate cookies and drank punch for Communion, I wasn't gonna get excited about it.

She cleared her throat, and the children sat as still as statues, waiting to hear from God. I stared hard at the smear of lipstick on the teacher lady's teeth.

"So as I was saying, Jesus taught us it isn't the amount

we contribute that's important. It's the attitude with which we give. He wants us to give from the heart and sacrifice more than what we're comfortable living without."

The kids squirmed. I picked my nose. I hoped we'd get to something interesting soon.

"There's a family in our congregation who've been going through a hard time. You all know the Smiths." The fifth graders nodded like robots.

I raised my hand again.

"Yes, Bernice?"

"What kind of hard time?" I asked. "They end up in jail?"

"Oh, heavens no. Mr. Smith lost his job and Mrs. Smith is sick in the hospital. They have four little mouths to feed."

"My momma got five mouths to feed, plus her own big fat one. And she don't got no job." The Buttmans weren't rolling in the dough, but everyone already knew that, so no use pretending we were. That was just the way it was.

The Sunday school teacher's cheeks turned awful pink then, and I wasn't exactly sure why.

"Today we're going to be taking up a collection to help the Smiths. I want you to give the way Jesus taught us, children." She passed a brown basket to the kid nearest her, and he dug in his pocket and pulled out a crumpled dollar bill and a baseball card. He dropped the dollar in the basket. But after catching the teacher's eye, he frowned and added the baseball card before passing the container to the next kid.

"That's wonderful. God sees your generosity. All the

other Sunday school classes took an offering this morning as well. I know the Smiths will be ever so grateful."

One kid pulled a twenty out of a stiff leather wallet and dropped it in. My jaw came unhinged. *Twenty bucks!*

I thought about all those other offering baskets in all those other Sunday school rooms. A metric crap-ton of cash. That amount of money would nearly fund my latest and greatest ambition.

I reached into the back pocket of my muddy jeans and unfolded the flyer I'd printed at the library for the Hollywood Hills Stunt Camp. As of last week, it was my life's dream to go to this camp and learn to sword-fight, jump out of helicopters, and punch people harder. Of course, I was only guessing about the details of the program. But it was in California, which was about a jillion miles from Kansas City and the Loser Trailer Park. (It was 1,624.6 miles to be exact. I'd Googled it.)

"What's that?" Oliver asked, peeking over my shoulder at the flyer. His breath smelled like pancakes and maple syrup. Lucky jerk.

I shoved the paper back in my pocket before he could get a good look at it.

"Nothing." I pinched him hard on the soft underside of his arm while the Sunday school teacher congratulated another kid on his generosity. Oliver stretched his face into a silent scream and rubbed the spot furiously. That was gonna leave a mark.

When the basket got to me, my fingers itched to snake that cash and make a run for it. Coins and wadded-up bills covered the bottom of the basket, and it pressed heavy on my lap. I bit the inside of my cheek, trying to resist the smash and grab.

The teacher put her hand on my shoulder. "It's touching, isn't it? People are good at heart. When asked to give, they always rise to the challenge." She lifted the basket from my lap and marched it to the back of the room.

For a hot minute I thought I heard angels singing, but then I realized it was just an amazing idea rolling around in my head.

3

Plan in Action

Darn the library for being closed on the Lord's Day. I had to wait until Monday after school to get my plan rolling. I entered the dim coolness of the ancient building and took in a noseful of dusty books and lemon furniture polish. That just might be my favorite smell in all the world.

There wasn't time to hang out and sniff, though. When I came to the library, I always tried to stay inconspicuous (that means out of sight). People might get the wrong idea if they saw Bernice Buttman spending time between stacks of books for fun. Bullies don't hang out at the library unless they're drawing devil horns on all the picture book characters.

I tossed my dirty black backpack under the computer desk and looked around like a kid with her mitt in the cookie jar. The handful of library-goers had their noses stuffed in books, so they didn't notice me. I turned to the dusty screen and moved the mouse to wake it up.

The first time I'd come here was the summer after first grade. Momma would kick us out of the trailer as soon as she woke up in the morning, and my brothers would ditch me to shoot BB guns at tin cans or sneak into the public pool. The library was on my short list of "places that have air conditioning and welcome loitering." In case you don't know, *loitering* is a big word for standing around and bugging real customers and not buying a thing.

Once the perky librarian, Ms. Knightley, had shown me how to look things up with a search engine, I was under her feet all the livelong day. Knowledge was only a click away. I could know *everything* if I asked enough questions. Which would mean I'd always be right. I'd taken to writing down questions in a green notebook I carried in my backpack, so I'd know what to ask when I got to the computer.

Now I took out the rippled notebook and looked at the previous week's page.

45. How to make cherry bombs
46. Why do I fart?
47. Why do dogs eat grass?

I flipped to the next page, where I'd only scrawled one question. It was a big one. Next summer's entire destiny depended on the answer.

"Hard at work there, Bernice?" Ms. Knightley leaned

against the edge of my cubicle, and I jumped. I snapped the notebook closed, and she raised her eyebrows.

"Yup. Tryin' to find out what makes Pop Rocks pop." *Oh, snap!* I grinned at my own fast thinking. That question wasn't even on my list! I'd add it later.

"Interesting. Let me know what you find." Ms. Knightley always asked me what I'd learned from my searches. She said I had a knack for research. No other adults ever said I had a knack for anything. Except my fourth-grade teacher, who'd said I had a way of making the simplest group project a nightmare.

I nodded at Ms. Knightley, and guilt twisted my guts. My plan wasn't exactly legit, and I was pretty sure I knew what she'd say about that. But if I was going to get to Hollywood Hills Stunt Camp this summer, I needed some generous strangers to dig down deep and give from their hearts.

Ms. Knightley still hovered nearby. Her hair is cut short like a pixie's, and she always wears sweaters, even in the summer, because she says the air conditioner gives her a chill.

She smiled and tilted her head to one side. "Is there anything you need to confess?" Her voice was quiet but with a sharp edge. My heart started banging around like a squirrel in the dryer, and I shoved my hands under the desk so that she couldn't see them shaking.

"Confess?" I squeaked. Normally I do bad things and

I don't feel bad about them. But Ms. Knightley makes me want to be a good person. I don't want her to look at me like a clump of mud on her shoe like everyone else does. I think she might actually like me. But that's probably because she's never seen me steal milk money from the kindergartners.

"You're holding out on me," she said, extending her hand.

I stared at her jangly bracelet and thought about handing the notebook over. I thought about slipping her a bribe. I thought about writing out a confession letter of everything bad I'd ever done and plopping it in Ms. Knightley's hand.

"Your gum, Bernice," Ms. Knightley said kindly. "You know the library's policy."

I let out a long breath and spit my hunk of Hubba Bubba right into her hand.

She winced a little bit, but her smile came right back. "Thank you. Let me know if you need any help."

She strolled back to the information desk, depositing my gum in a trash can along the way.

I took a deep breath and turned back to the waiting search bar. My fingers flew across the keys as I typed my question, and I scratched some notes in my notebook. This didn't look that hard. It almost looked *too* easy.

If stunt camp was gonna be in my future, I would need a round-trip bus ticket, plus payment for camp. And some money for snacks and smoke bombs. Subtract out the twenty-two dollars in my savings account (I'd opened it when I turned eight with the twenty-dollar bill my aunt had sent me), and that meant I had to scrounge up just under two thousand five hundred dollars. I was too young for a job (plus who in the world would hire me?), and Momma would laugh in my face if I asked her. I had to come up with the money on my own. But I had a plan.

I would get people to give me the money. Just like when they passed the basket around in Sunday school. It would be as easy as shaking down the kindergartners.

First, I went to a website called Fund Me Up! and set up a fake profile. I stared at the screen for a minute, thinking about what kind of person other people wanted to help. Nice families, like the Smiths from church, usually got people's attention. Or maybe a sick kid? I'd probably need to know all about some kind of disease for that to work, though.

Then it hit me up side my head, like my brother Busey does when he catches me wiping boogers on his pillow.

People go nuts for dogs. Puppies. Little sick puppies.

Google gave me just what I needed, and ten minutes later my charity was live. I leaned back in my chair and clicked on the page to view it like everyone else would.

At the top of the screen was the picture I'd found when I searched for "ugly dogs." The mutt had actually won some contests for being so unattractive. He was a small brown dog with mismatched, crossed eyes, a few snaggly teeth, and a tongue that hung out the side of his mouth. I'd named my pretend dog Farkle, and the heading at the top of the page read "Help Farkle Smile Again." In the description section I'd written a heart-tugging story about how I'd found Farkle in a sewer pipe near my house and the vet said he needed surgery to make his tongue go inside his mouth instead of lolling out. I set the goal amount of the fund for two thousand four hundred ninety-seven dollars and sat back, congratulating myself for my genius.

The only thing that made me cringe was my real name at the bottom of the page. I had to use my real name so the money raised would go in my real bank account. But it seemed pretty risky putting the Buttman name on anything I needed people's cooperation with.

I stared at the ugly dog and prayed no one would notice his owner. He did seem like the kind of dog my family would have, anyway. And the more I stared at his hairy little face, the more I felt like the two of us could be kin.

I glanced up as Ms. Knightley helped a preschool kid find a book. Probably a book about fire trucks, because the kid wanted to be a firefighter when he grew up. She'd tell him he absolutely could, even though he was a scrawny little wimp. She always tells kids they can be whatever they want to be.

If I decided I wanted to be a Hollywood stuntwoman and I told Ms. Knightley, she'd glow with excitement.

She'd tell me to chase my dreams and give me a stack of books about being a stuntwoman.

But I wasn't sure what I wanted to be when I grew up. It all seemed like a lot of hard work: finishing school, getting a job. All I really knew was I wanted to get out of the trailer and away from Momma. I wanted a break from my smelly older brothers. I wanted to learn how to ride a camel backward while shooting at low-flying airplanes.

Ms. Knightley might not approve of my fundraising methods, but she would want me to chase my dream. Bernice Buttman was gonna be the star of Hollywood Hills Stunt Camp, just so long as nobody recognized that ugly mutt.

4

Bringing Up Buttmans

By the time I rolled past the Lone Star Trailer Park mailboxes, the sky was deep purple, like a bruise. I threw my bike in the front yard, next to the garden trolls and the cast-iron bathtub full of weeds, and clumped up the path to our Palace on Wheels, as Momma called it.

"There's Bernice! She can be the judge!" The voice belonged to my oldest brother, Austin, but I couldn't figure out where in the blazes he was.

I stood frozen to the spot, looking in every direction for my pack of brothers. You didn't want them sneaking up on you, that's for sure. An empty bottle of Mountain Dew clunked me in the head, and I yelped in pain before spotting the dark outline of four huge lumps on the roof of the trailer.

"Dang it, Chucknorris. I said toss it near her, not brain-damage her! Come around back, Bernice. We got a job for you." There have been times in the past when my brothers have conned me into doing things that were probably not all that smart. But they were always fun, and curiosity usually won out. Austin's wicked grin almost glowed in the dark, so I tromped through the brown grass to the backyard and nearly ran into a huge trampoline.

"Whoa! Where'd you get this?" I yelled.

"Don't worry about that," Austin said. He was a senior in high school, and most of my brothers' worst ideas came from him. "We need you to give us scores on our jumpin'."

I crossed my arms and crushed my eyebrows together. Jumping off the roof? The trailer groaned under their combined weight. There was no way that trampoline would be able to snap back from an airborne Buttman.

"I don't think that's—"

"Look out below!" Gordon said, flinging himself off the roof and sinking deep in the center of the trampoline before crashing into the brown grass of the neighbor's yard with a thump.

"Woo-hoo! That's what I'm talking about!" Chucknorris said. "What's Gordo's score, Bernice?"

Gordon moaned from the neighbor's yard, but he waved to let us know he was okay. "Um, seven?"

"Watch and learn, little brothers," Austin said. "This is how Stone Cold Austin Buttman does it!" He looked like a meteor hurtling at the ground, but he did manage to stay on the trampoline. It sprang him high as the trailer, and when he was done bouncing, he lay on the trampoline and laughed his head off. Chucknorris and Busey clapped and cheered from the roof. I gave Austin a nine.

"A nine?" he grumbled. "That was a thing of beauty."

"You lost a point for your butt crack showing." I shrugged. Austin put me in a headlock.

"Baby brother's turn!" Austin yelled up to Busey. He might be the baby brother, but he was the tallest and widest of any of us. He hitched up his pants with determination before flinging himself off the roof.

And broke the legs right off the trampoline.

He lay there on the tangle of black fabric and bent-up metal poles and for a second no one moved.

"I'm okay!" he said weakly, which sent all of us into a fresh round of applause. It also ended the game. Chucknorris seemed relieved he didn't have to jump. By the time he'd climbed down the back side of the trailer, he was sweaty and red.

"Y'all are lucky I didn't get to jump," he mumbled. "I woulda wiped the floor with you."

• • • •

Momma and her boyfriend, Lloyd, were watching TV when I followed my limping brothers through the front door. She didn't look up from her plate of microwave burritos or the reality TV show she was glued to. Lloyd only nodded at us.

"Hey, Momma," the boys said, filing past her to go scrounge up some dinner.

"Hey yourselves. Thank God you're done making that racket. I thought the roof was gonna rain down on my head." Momma shifted her plate, which was balanced on her NASCAR T-shirt. She called it her belly shelf.

Lloyd scratched and let out an enormous burp, and I chuckled. Momma gave him a punch in the arm. "That smelled like pork rinds. Blow it the other way next time."

"You like it." Lloyd rubbed his almost-bald head and leaned back in the recliner. His white tank top was scattered with BBQ stains, like a fairy had fallen, butt-over-elbows, all down the front of him.

Momma let out a sigh, which was directed at the TV. "This show is terrible. Who wants to watch people survive in the jungle? They need to make a show about *us.*"

My brothers returned from the kitchen with bags of chips and sloppy peanut-butter-and-Marshmallow-Fluff sandwiches. Austin got the La-Z-Boy, and the rest of us plopped down on the floor in front of the TV.

"Being on TV is my life's dream," Momma said, her mouth full of burrito. "*Bringing Up Buttmans* would've been a smash hit." Momma's frown made her look like she had about a million chins.

"Oh, not again," I grumbled.

"All family reality shows need a cute kid. We've missed our window." Momma's eyes shot laser beams at me.

"I can't help it if I'm grown! Maybe it was because you tried to rap in all your audition videos!"

"Don't you sass your mouth at me, missy." Momma set her empty plate down on the couch. "Those tapes were golden. I bet nobody important ever saw them, though. And now we don't got an ounce of cute in this house, so my dream is gonna curl up and die."

She was right there. They'd have to be crazy to put our ugly family on TV. But Momma never thinks about anything else.

"I was born to be famous," she sighed. Lloyd nodded in agreement.

"There ain't no one deserves it more than you, sugar."

Lloyd's been around for about a year now, and I guess we're all kinda getting used to him. He's okay as long as you don't sit downwind of him. None of us know our real daddies, anyway. Momma named the boys after the celebrities that most closely resembled their fathers. She named me after her great-grandma. Lucky me. I'd have rather been named Kidrock Buttman (after my daddy's look-alike) over Bernice any day.

Chucknorris and Busey started punching each other and rolling around on the floor. Busey wasn't acting right, and I wondered if landing flat on his back had given his brains a jiggle.

Lloyd and Momma argued about what show to watch

next, and Austin and Gordon snuck out the back door in all the chaos. Probably to go cause more chaos.

I looked around at this mess of people that were supposed to be my family and wondered if I really and truly did fit in here. When I grew up, was I gonna turn into an exact replica of Momma, complete with bad attitude and mean spirit? I was a Buttman, after all, and I didn't think it was in any way avoidable. I thought about Farkle, my imaginary pet dog, and I smiled. This summer I'd be on a bus to California. I would be greeted at stunt camp by piles of new friends. I'd win them over with the variety of songs I could play with only my armpits, and my ability to perform every stunt perfectly on the first try. The rest of the Buttmans would be stuck here in the Lone Star until the end of time, and they could kiss my grits.

5

Curiosity Killed the Wimp

I checked Fund Me Up! at the library every day that week and watched the red progress bar get closer and closer to the goal. It was working. My plan was actually working. The only comments people had left on the page were nice.

"Hope Farkle is smiling soon!"

"Good luck with your operation, doggie!"

"What a sweet dog! I bet he has a wonderful personality."

I snorted at that last one. I was booger-eating proof that just because you're ugly, don't mean you automatically get a wonderful personality.

"Bernice? Is that you?"

I turned around slowly in my chair and saw Oliver staring at me in that openmouthed way he had. I wondered if he swallowed many flies, what with his barn door open all the time.

He was so short we were practically eye-to-eye even

though I was sitting and he was standing. That's when I realized he wasn't looking me in the eye at all. He was staring at the blasted computer screen right over my shoulder.

"Whoa. Is that your dog?" he asked, leaning in. I could smell brownies on his breath. Didn't his mother do anything except stuff him with delicious food?

"No."

"Why's your name on there, then?" Oliver squinted and pushed his glasses farther up his nose.

"Oh, um. Yeah." I swallowed hard, my throat suddenly tight. My name might as well have been blinking at the bottom of the web page.

"Gosh. He looks special. Why's he have his own web page? Does he blog or something?"

I ducked and weaved, trying to get my body between Oliver and the computer screen, but he was like a snoopy ninja. Sure, you get one imaginary dog and then all of a sudden people come out of nowhere to have a chat. It was the worst possible time, what with my lies on full display, but at least Oliver was talking to me. Maybe there was hope that we could be buddies.

"And he has to have surgery! That's terrible. My granny just had a surgery on her heart. She died."

I stared at him, eyes bugged out and nostrils flared. What was I supposed to say to that? A friend would probably try and say something comforting, but my mind was drawing a big old blank. I just wanted Oliver to go away so I could close the web page before he blabbed to everyone that Farkle was mine.

Oliver must have misread my awkwardness for worry about my fake dog. "But I'm sure Farkle will be just fine." He patted my arm but then backed quickly away. Huh. Kind of nice.

I turned around and clicked off the web page, but my heart was skitterin' in my chest. Help me, Jesus. Oliver knew too much.

6

The Thousand-Dollar Jackpot

The smell of oil and gasoline hit me in the schnoz as soon as I walked into the trailer, and *Family Guy* blared on the TV. I had to step over the engine parts scattered across the living room floor. Lloyd crouched next to the reeking engine, wrench in hand, mouth hanging slack like Oliver's.

"Where is everybody?" I asked.

"Momma went to buy her lottery ticket, and your chucklehead brothers went to go tip over porta-potties at the construction site."

I grinned and hoped one of them would videotape it.

I headed to the screened-in porch, which served as my bedroom as long as the weather cooperated. It was only big enough to fit the musty green couch I slept on and some cardboard boxes full of junk that didn't belong anywhere else. I looked around and frowned. Nothing about this room reminded me of myself. Except it was ugly.

My brothers shared a room, with two sets of bunk beds crammed about as tight as possible under the low ceilings. It stunk in there.

Momma and Lloyd had the only other bedroom. Momma said she was counting down the days until our sorry selves were out of school and out of her hair. I guess if we graduated we had to move out. Good thing there was a very small chance of that happening.

My brothers continued to pass school because they were so close in age, if one of them flunked, some poor teacher would have two of them in the same class, and nobody would suggest that. So the Buttman boys kept moving up, but I'm pretty sure all of them had beans for brains.

I could do fine in school if I wanted to. Most days I didn't find bookwork too appealing, is all. And there were always wimps to punish, and detentions to sleep through. I didn't believe I'd need to know algebra if I became a Hollywood stuntwoman, anyway.

The front door slammed, and I heard Momma growl, "Where is she?"

I gulped, being the only other "she" in the family. I tried to think of all the misdemeanors I'd committed in the last few days, but none of them seemed like anything Momma would get so worked up about. Her footsteps crashed down the hallway, and I winced as she threw open the aluminum door and sent it slamming into the side of the Palace on Wheels.

I jumped up off my couch-bed, prepared to fling myself out one of the screen walls if I needed to.

"Bernice!" she yelled, jowls quivering. "You have done it this time!" She yanked my arm, nearly popping it out of the socket, and I flopped around like a rag doll. I saved all my fight-back for school.

"Wh-what are you t-talking about?" I stuttered. She squeezed my arm hard, and I could picture her sausage fingers smushing through my biceps like soft cheese.

"You know what I'm talking about. People were whispering at every end of the convenience store. They *smiled* at me."

And then I knew.

The website.

Farkle.

I was in big trouble.

"Sandy Kifner came up to me while I picked my five and handed me a twenty." She paused so I could squirm. "For our poor sick dog, Farkle."

I could feel my face blazing. Sandy Kifner lives right next door to Oliver and is best friends with his mom. The two of them gossip like it's going out of style.

"Um . . . did you want to give me the twenty?" I squeaked.

Momma's laugh was cruel. "If stupid could fly, you'd be a jet, Bernice. You made up some story 'bout a sick dog to get people to give you money?"

"A website."

"How much money have you stolen?"

I winced at the word *stolen.* In my mind, that money was *donations.* Not that I was above stealing, but I'd made a distinction in my brain.

"I . . . I'm not sure," I said, jutting out my chin.

"Tell me." Momma's foul breath was so close to my face, I nearly gagged.

"Last I checked it was one thousand three hundred and seventy-five dollars."

Momma and I locked eyes and it was quiet as wool socks on carpet.

A smile started to spread across her face. "Well. Ain't you slicker than a greased hog. Hot dang! Today is my lucky day." She let go of my arm and I rubbed at the sore spot.

"You're talking crazy." I sank into the stinky couch. "Didn't Sandy Kifner know we ain't got no dog?"

"She sure didn't. And neither does anyone else, which is why you're gonna take down that website and hand over the cash to me, and in exchange I won't call the authorities."

"What? No! I'm not giving you my money."

"Your money! Ain't that rich? Did you know it's a *felony* to set up a fake charity online?"

I gulped and closed my eyes.

"That's right. Momma can use the computers at the library, too."

I pictured her walking into my sacred library space, and I wanted to hurl. Somehow the fake wood cubicles and the quiet tunnels of books didn't feel as safe if Momma was allowed to walk in there anytime she wanted. Was it true, about it being a felony what I'd done? Why hadn't I bothered to Google that in the beginning?

She began to laugh, a low sick chuckle. "Know what I did with the twenty bucks?"

I shook my head.

"Bought me some more pick fives. Didn't win a red cent. Until now, that is. I just won a thousand-dollar jackpot."

7

A Fate Worse Than Head Lice

The next time Oliver asked me about Farkle, I gave him a purple nurple. I drifted through the following days like a Twinkie wrapper blowing through a parking lot. My savings account was as empty as the day was long, including the twenty dollars I'd gotten for my birthday. Momma called it a stupid tax and included it with the rest of the money I'd raised.

She was as happy as a bird peckin' a french fry, and I tried to avoid her at home as much as possible. There was no hope of stunt camp, no hope of a summer away from the trailer park, and no going to California where no one knew a single Buttman.

Momma caught me heading out the door on Saturday morning with my arms full of eggs.

"Where you think you're going?" She stood between me and the door.

"Nowhere." I tried to slip the carton of eggs behind my back and one of them squeezed out and plopped on the floor.

"You were heading to the overpass to toss eggs at cars." It wasn't even a question. Our eyes locked and it was like I dared her to tell me not to go. That would make going even more enjoyable.

"I need to talk to you, Bernice."

My stomach flopped like a sackful of rattlesnakes. I was only eleven years old, but in my experience, when someone tells you they need to talk, it's never about how they wanna shower you with candy and cheese balls.

"Lloyd and me . . . Well, I've decided I need to make a move. For my career."

I scratched my head. *Career?*

"There's these open auditions in Los Angeles. This could be my big break!"

My face lit up like a Christmas tree. "We're movin'! To California? Hot dang!" Swimming pools, movie stars, and . . . stunt camp!

Momma stepped forward then and put her hand on my arm. "No, Bernice. Me and Lloyd are moving to California."

My throat started closing up, and I wondered if maybe I'd accidentally swallowed a rock. I opened my mouth and snapped it shut again and again.

"Your brothers will stay here. They can take care of themselves. But you require some supervision. . . ."

Another egg plopped out of the carton behind my back, and I winced as it hit the floor.

"So where will I go?" I couldn't think of one single person who'd welcome me to come live with them. Shoot, my own family was about to kick me out.

"You're gonna go live at Aunt Josephine's." She crossed her arms like it was a done deal.

"I never even met Aunt Josephine!"

"Oh, Bernice, stop being dramatic. You met Josephine when you were five. You don't remember because she gave you a toy, and you took the nine-volt batteries out of it and stuck them on your tongue. Probably fried your brains."

Sticking batteries on my tongue sounded familiar. In fact, my tongue buzzed with the memory. But I didn't remember anything else about my aunt. Except . . .

My face must have gone as white as a sun-bleached dishrag. "Wait . . . isn't she a *nun*?"

"She's barely a nun. I mean, she wears the whole outfit and has some old-lady roommates, but there are only like ten Catholics in that town, so I hardly think it counts."

So that was it, then. My momma thought I would go and live with the nuns while she chased her Hollywood dreams. Well, she had another think coming.

• • • •

The library was cool and quiet as I slipped in the door and headed to my computer cubicle. I'd left the eggs splattered on the trailer floor while Momma packed her bags for a Hollywood adventure. *My* Hollywood adventure.

She tried to tell me it would be temporary. As soon as her and Lloyd got jobs on a TV show, they'd come back for me. Momma even said if I stopped whining about it and stayed out of trouble she might pay me back. I wasn't gonna hold my breath.

There was no way they were gonna get me to go, pure and simple. I'd have Austin or one of the other knuckleheads drive me around the trailer park until Momma and Lloyd left, and then I'd stay at the Lone Star with my brothers.

Except Momma had already talked to Aunt Josephine, and she expected me next week. She'd probably do the right thing and call Momma when I didn't arrive (didn't nuns always do the right thing?).

The more I thought about it, the angrier I got, and there weren't any other kids around to pound. Instead, I banged my head against the wooden computer desk.

Thump, thump, thump.

"Bernice, what on earth is the matter?" Ms. Knightley pulled a chair up next to mine, and her hand hovered over my back. I laid my face down on the table and squeezed my eyes shut. One traitor tear managed to squeeze out.

"Nothin'."

"You can tell me, you know. We're friends, aren't we?"

The funny thing was, Ms. Knightley was the closest thing I had to a friend. She always seemed happy to see me, and she didn't think of me as "one of those awful Buttmans."

And then someone waved the checkered flag and all the words came speeding out of me like race cars.

"My momma is giving me away. Or sending me away. To live with my aunt in a dumb small town. And she's a nun!"

Ms. Knightley's mouth froze in the shape of an O, and I watched as she tried to pull herself back together.

"Your mother is a nun?"

I let out a sigh. "No. My aunt is a nun. And I have to go live with her."

"You're moving," Ms. Knightley stated, tilting her head so that our faces could look straight at each other.

"Oh no I'm not! She can't make me! I'll figure out a way to stay."

Ms. Knightley drummed her fingers on the desk in front of me and bit her bottom lip.

"But what if you didn't?"

"Didn't what?"

"Stay here. What if you *did* go live in a new town with new people?"

"I'd hate it. I'd miss it here."

Ms. Knightley's mouth scrunched into a little bow. "What would you miss?"

I listened to the clock ticking. And ticking. And ticking. What would I miss?

I sure as all get-out wouldn't miss any of those kids at my school, who treated me like a plague victim they needed to avoid to survive. I wouldn't miss the teachers, who always assumed I didn't know nothing just because I'm a Buttman. I wouldn't miss Lloyd, taking his dumb engines apart on the living room floor. I wouldn't miss Momma hollering at me day and night.

Ms. Knightley still stared at me, waiting for an answer.

I shrugged. "I guess nothing."

"Maybe your favorite librarian?" she said, winking at me.

I smiled. "Yeah, maybe just you."

"Bernice, I know you may not believe what I'm about to say, but this *might* be the best thing that's ever happened to you."

I sat up and wiped my face.

"What do you mean?"

"Going to live in a new place is starting over. It's like a clean slate." She had the softest kind of smile on her face, and it made my guts ache.

"Maybe I don't want to start over." I scowled again.

She tapped her perfectly painted fingernails on the desk like she was having a very wise thought. "Sometimes it's the people around us who help us figure out who we are. This is your chance to learn from some new people."

I crossed my arms like a pretzel. I already knew who

I was. Bernice Buttman. Cheese ball eater. Kindergarten money stealer. Sunday school terrorizer. Mini-version of my momma.

But was that who I had to be? Who I wanted to be?

What if Ms. Knightley was right and there was a whole other version of me that just needed a little space to grow? My shoulders slumped. "Maybe you're right."

"I'm a librarian. I'm rarely wrong."

I stood up and started to walk away but turned back to Ms. Knightley. "Would it be okay if I emailed you from time to time? Just to see how the library's holding up without me?"

Ms. Knightley beamed. "Of course. I'd like that very much." She walked over to a shelf in the children's section and picked up a well-worn book, thumbed through the pages, and handed it to me.

"*Where the Sidewalk Ends*, by Shel Silverstein," I read. "What's this?"

"Read the part that's marked." She smiled, all dimply and twinkly.

"*Anything can happen, child. Anything can be.*" The words hung in the air like a promise, and I nodded and handed the book back.

A new beginning. A new adventure.

Too bad the only book quote that kept dashing through my head was *There's no place like home. There's no place like home.*

8

Halfway to Nowhere

Chucknorris volunteered to drop me off, since he'd only just got his license and hardly ever got to use the beat-up Ford truck the boys shared. I had my doubts about that junker getting us there without coughing black fumes and leaving us on the side of the road.

My brother smiled hard as he messed with the radio and dangled his ham-hock arm out the window. *Too dang happy.* I licked my finger and stuck it right in his ear.

Freakin' traitor.

"Whaddya do that for?" He swerved the truck, clawing at the side of his head, and then punched me in the arm.

"Aren't you a teeny bit sad Momma's abandoning me to the wolves?"

"They're nuns, not wolves."

I pressed my forehead against the window's cool glass. "I think I'd rather take my chances with wolves."

"It'll be all right, sis. You're tough." Chucknorris could

be a real sweetheart when he wanted to be. He almost never wanted to be, though.

A few hours went by with my brother banging his head to the radio and singing along when he knew the words. And also when he didn't. After he belted out a loud chorus of "We built this city on sausage rolls!" I finally leaned over and snapped off the music.

"Where is this place, anyway?" My heart bumped around like soda cans tied to a bumper. *I'm moving, and I don't even know the name of the town in my new address.* Momma had said things like "three hours away" and "just a little south," but for some reason I'd never thought to ask *where*.

Chucknorris scratched his hairy armpit, one hand still on the wheel. "Town's called Halfway," he snorted.

"Halfway? Halfway to where?"

"Halfway to darn near nowhere, s'what it looks like."

It was true. We'd exited the highway a few miles back, and all we could see were cows and the occasional farmhouse. We lived pretty far from downtown, so it's not like I'd never seen a cow before, but there also weren't many wide-open spaces in the Lone Star Trailer Park.

The speed limit slowed to twenty, and Chucknorris pointed out a sign for the Halfway Baptist Church. We got a good laugh out of that. Must be for people who didn't want the commitment of being all-the-way Baptist.

We rounded a corner and the rest of the town unfolded in front of us. It was real pretty, like a postcard town. Big trees lined the main street, dotting the road with shadows and light. The storefronts were small and neat and had hand-painted signs that read FRANK'S DINER and SAL'S HARDWARE. I couldn't see a Walmart or a Burger King anywhere.

Chucknorris let out a low whistle. "Not too shabby."

I crossed my arms. Who cared what the town looked like? I was still me, and I didn't belong here.

My brother checked the address scrawled on the back of a receipt and pulled up to the last building on the end of the street. The church was a small, whitewashed building, with a steeple and a cross decorating the red roof. Two arched windows sparkled on either side of the double doors, and some hanging flower baskets shifted in the breeze. The sign out front read ST. DROGO'S CATHOLIC CHURCH AND ABBEY. I whipped out my green notebook and copied *St. Drogo* down. I had lots of questions about him.

Chucknorris let the truck idle. I guessed he wasn't in the mood for a long goodbye. He hopped out and plucked my battered suitcase from the truck bed, flinging it at me as I shut the passenger door.

"This is your stop." He wouldn't look me in the eyes.

I couldn't keep myself from being a sap. I ran over and wrapped my arms around my big dumb brother's belly. His shirt smelled bad, but he started blinking extra fast and he still wouldn't look me in the eyes. "Can't believe I'm just 'sposed to leave you here," he mumbled, rumpling my hair.

I squeezed him again extra tight. He patted me and said, "Come on. Get yourself together, kid." But he was the one blubbering like a baby!

"You said I'd be just fine, remember?"

He nodded. "You've got my number. Your big brothers still got your back. Just give us a holler if you need us."

With one last wave, he jumped back into the rust bucket and left me in a cloud of dust before I'd trudged up the red-brick pathway.

My legs wanted to make a run for it. I could camp in cow pastures and steal food from convenience stores. But then I remembered the book Ms. Knightley had shown me.

Anything can happen, child, anything can be.

I took a deep breath and rang the doorbell, which set off a whole choir of bells playing a churchy song I didn't recognize. It sounded real nice, and I would've been happy standing there, listening to the tune while gripping my ratty suitcase (which contained every blasted thing I owned). But just then, the double doors swung open.

The woman (lady? sister? nun?) standing before me had as many chins as Momma. I didn't have a spare second to inspect the rest of her face because before I knew it she crushed me in a squashy, sweet-smelling hug.

"Good heavens!" she said, holding me at arm's length.

"You're just as pretty as the day is long. Come on in, girl, and let's show you around."

Huh. Not the usual first impression of me. Did this lady need glasses? Also, who the heck was she?

My confusion must've reached my face, because the sister extended her hand all formal-like and said, "I'm your aunt Josephine. But people here call me Sister Mary Margaret."

I swallowed hard and nodded. Even though she was huggy, and fast and loose with the compliments, I had to keep my head. I wasn't going to like her, or anything else about Halfway, and that was that. My heart did a weird bumpy rhythm and I gripped the suitcase handle tighter.

"You're Bernice?"

"Yup."

We stood there awkwardly for a second before she turned on her heels and led the way into the dim church. "Welcome home."

"This ain't my home," I said under my breath. It wasn't anyone's home, actually. It was a church, not too different from the one I'd crashed only weeks before. The ceiling was high and crisscrossed with wooden beams. Exactly eight pews lined the walls. What could that hold, like twenty people? Only if they were skinny. Narrow windows, high up, let the afternoon light stretch across the floor. A plain table stood at the front of the room, draped with a white cloth, and a small Jesus-on-the-cross hung behind it.

My new guardian had already disappeared, and I stood there, gripping my suitcase and shifting my weight. This whole thing was nuttier than a porta-potty at a peanut festival.

"You coming?" Her voice drifted from behind a door off to the side of the entry. I pushed it slowly, expecting . . . I don't know what I was expecting. But it turned out to be a regular old set of stairs, lit by a bare lightbulb dangling from a chain. The stairs ended in a brightly lit walk-out basement set up as a kind of apartment.

My aunt stood in front of a large wooden kitchen table, with a freakin' huge smile on her face. I dropped my stuff in the middle of the floor and took a few cautious steps.

There wasn't much to look at. The table took up most of the kitchen. White cabinets wrapped around a refrigerator and stove. No microwave anywhere. How'd they cook burritos?

An old plaid couch stood facing a bookshelf crammed with ancient-looking books, and a kind of stitched-up picture of Jesus hung on the wall. There was no TV.

NO TV.

The silence of the no TV was deafening. My palms got sweaty and blood pounded in my ears. What did people do all day if they didn't have a TV?

Only three doors connected to the main rooms. Two more nuns came out of one of them. They reminded me of penguins waddling along in their black outfits.

Josephine cheerfully dipped her head at them. "Sisters! Our guest is here! Meet my niece Bernice. Oh, niece-Bernice! That rhymes. . . ."

I waggled my fingers at them in a wave, then crossed my arms to avoid more handshaking or hugging.

The tiniest nun approached me first. She was much older than the other two, her skin so papery thin and wrinkled I had the urge to run my fingertips along the creases. She smiled, and her pale blue eyes 'bout got buried up in all those crinkles.

The other sister stepped forward and put her arm on the tiny one's shoulder. "This is Sister Angela-Clarence. Forgive her . . . her mind has gone a bit these last few years."

My aunt gave me a reassuring smile. "She only speaks in children's book quotes. Doesn't make a lick of sense most of the time. Just smile and nod."

I smiled and nodded at the old nun. She leaned in and whispered, "*I knew who I was this morning, but I've changed a few times since then.*"

Aunt Josephine rubbed her chin. "I think that was from *Alice in Wonderland.*"

The younger nun stepped forward. "I'm Sister Marie Francis. Pleased to meet you, Bernice."

She stuck out her hand and I shook it. Marie Francis was around my momma's age. She had straight teeth and a crooked nose. Her hands were rough and large. She smelled sorta like outside. Like grass and wind and sunshine.

"Are there any more of you? That live here, I mean?"

"Nope. You're looking at the complete roster of St. Drogo's Abbey. We are few, but we are mighty." She flung her arms around the other two like they were posing for a picture.

"Let's show Bernice around," Sister Marie Francis said, grabbing my hand and pulling me to the door they'd just come out of.

She flicked on the light, and I blinked a few times to adjust to the brightness. Two sets of bunk beds crammed in there, and not much else. Plain brown blankets were smoothed over the beds. A lone picture of a sad lady with a shiny head hung on the wall. It was as crowded as my brothers' room, except it smelled better.

My aunt (was I supposed to call her Sister Mary Margaret?) said, "This is our room. No frills or thrills in here."

I nodded and backed out of the small space with everyone else.

"This door's the bathroom," she continued, and they all stood at a respectful distance as I stuck my head in the room and nodded at the sink, toilet, and shower.

Only one door in this tiny space hadn't been opened yet. I guessed it was some sort of broom closet they'd thrown a cot in for me.

"And this will be your room while you're here." Marie Francis flung the last door open and cracked a smile.

This room was larger, or maybe it just looked that way because it only had one twin bed pressed against the wall. A patchwork quilt covered the bed, and two fluffy pillows in clean white cases rested on top. A doll sat propped up on the bed, its plastic eyes staring. I hadn't played with a doll in years (my brothers kept popping their heads off, on purpose and by accident). Some posters of kittens and puppies were thumbtacked to the walls, and a few empty shelves waited to be filled. In one corner sat a small desk with a set of stationery and a cup of pencils. And drawing me to it, like a skeeter to a bug zapper, was an ancient-looking computer.

The nuns studied my expression, and when my eyes reached the computer, Sister Marie Francis clapped her hands. "Everything in here was specially donated by St. Drogo's patrons. They wanted to make you feel at home here in Halfway."

The word *home* jerked me out of my stare-and-drool. Home was the Lone Star, with the Buttmans.

But it couldn't hurt to check out the computer.

"Does this work?" I ran my fingers along the keyboard. I itched to Google something. I'd never had my own computer, not even on loan. In fact, I'd never had a room with a bed before.

My aunt answered. "Mr. Jenkins says it works fine, and we had him hook it up to the internet. He's the principal at the Halfway Primary School. He said fifth graders do some of their homework online. We wanted to make sure you had everything you needed."

I had to blink my eyes real hard then, and I felt a golf-ball-sized lump choke my throat. It seemed crazy that strangers had opened their home to me and gone out of their way to make me feel welcome. Nobody ever tried to help me, except Ms. Knightley. It felt . . . *nice.*

The ancient Sister Angela-Clarence put her hand on my shoulder then and said, "*It is when we are most lost that we sometimes find our truest friends.*"

I gave Aunt Josephine a questioning look. "I think that one was from *Snow White*," she said thoughtfully.

I smiled and let the words plant themselves in my brain.

I sure hoped they were right.

9

Blank Slate

It turns out St. Drogo is the patron saint of ugly people. I'm not making that up. The web page said, "During a journey he was afflicted with a horrible disease. He became so terribly mutilated that he scared the townspeople." Boy, did that sound familiar.

I kept telling myself things could be different in Halfway. I could be different. No one knew me, or my family. I'd never threatened to push anyone's nose in dog doo here or stolen any milk money. This was the beginning of a new Bernice. I might even make up a new last name.

My aunt had promised to walk me to school on my first day, and Sister Marie Francis cooked up a big old pot of oatmeal for breakfast. I would rather eat the wood chips out of a hamster's cage than oatmeal, but I choked some down to be nice. (I was becoming a New and Improved Bernice already!) The horrible thought occurred to me that maybe the nuns had taken a vow of icky foods. I hadn't seen a cheese ball since I got here.

It put me in a cold sweat.

We walked out the front doors, but instead of heading down the road, Aunt Josephine steered me toward the back of the church. A dirt path wound through some high grass, and we stepped carefully toward a rickety wood fence. Horses stomped behind it, coats all shiny in the sun. They stuck their heads between the wide boards to eat the taller grass on our side.

"Those the neighbor's horses?" I asked. I didn't look at her, and I hoped she didn't hear the interest in my voice.

"Nope. They're ours. The sisters have had horses since St. Drogo's opened its doors in 1912."

Just then a blur of black and brown streaked across the pasture. Hooves pounded the dirt, and the ground rumbled. I craned my neck to watch as Sister Marie Francis and a chestnut horse flew over a fallen log. Her head covering flapped out behind her, her fists clutching the reins. The nun and the horse disappeared over a hill, and I let out a shaky breath.

"What. Was. That." I leaned against the fence, trying to steady myself from the weird adrenaline rush I'd just gotten.

My aunt adjusted her head thing (I needed to Google what those were called). "Sister Marie Francis has a history with horses. I'm sure she'd love to tell you about it sometime."

We walked along the fence line until it took a hard right and a road opened up. Just a ways farther and the Halfway Primary School stood in front of us, playground swarming with kids. I stopped on the sidewalk, gripping the straps of my backpack and gritting my teeth.

Anything can happen, child, anything can be.

My aunt turned my shoulders to face her and looked me right in the eyes. "You'll be fine, Bernice. Everyone's going to love you. Just be yourself."

Ha. Good one. My strategy was to try and be as far from myself as possible. New and improved me. Bionic me. Staying out of trouble and somehow raising money for stunt camp me.

• • • •

The first person I saw when I walked into Mr. Newton's fifth-grade class was Mr. Newton himself. He leaned back in his chair, behind a big metal desk, and ate a Pop-Tart from a paper plate balanced on his giant belly. Belly shelf, just like Momma. I smiled, even though I was more shook up than a Mountain Dew in a bike basket.

He stood when he saw me, and tossed the paper plate of crummies in the trash. He had one of those mustaches that curled up on the ends, and he wore suspenders and a bow tie.

The walls of the classroom were decorated with *Lord of the Rings* and *Game of Thrones* posters. The smell of coffee wafted through the air, and I hoped it was a fresh-brewed cup and not Mr. Newton's breath.

He wasn't smiling.

"Bernice Buttman?" he asked, peering at a file through round glasses.

Shoot. Permanent file. So much for forging a new identity.

Only three other kids milled around the room so far (the morning bell hadn't rung yet), and they all snickered at my name. I took a deep breath and tried to plaster on a smile, but it slid off my face quick as snot on spandex. Being nice to jerks was going to take some real muscle.

"That's me." My voice had a hard edge to it that cut the giggling off at the knees.

"You can take a seat right there in the back of the room." He didn't look at me, but squirted a glob of sanitizer in his hands and rubbed them together furiously.

I plopped down behind the only desk missing one of those taped-on name tags. A blond girl in the front row shot her hand in the air.

"Mr. Newton? Excuse me, Mr. Newton?"

The teacher flinched at the girl's voice.

"What is it, Imogene?" He sounded tired.

"Would you like me to show Bernice Buttman around? I could be like a sort of ambassador."

He straightened his bow tie as the morning bell rang and more students filed into the classroom. "I suppose so."

The girl gave me a sour smile before turning toward the front of the room. I clenched my fists under my desk and tried to think about stunt camp. Hang gliding. Dog-sledding. Target practice.

A folded-up note got to me during the middle of attendance. The blond girl had turned to stare at me again. I unfolded the pink notebook paper and got a whiff of strawberries. The purple ink had one sentence in perfect swooping cursive.

See you at lunch, Buttman.

I managed to stay mostly invisible for the first part of the day. My head swam thinking about all the catching up they wanted me to do. I'd have to read and study every day after school. But then I remembered my cozy little room at the convent, and my ancient computer that linked me to Google, and I figured, *Hey, what else do I have to do?*

Before I knew it, the lunch bell rang, and Imogene linked arms with me like we were best friends.

The school cafeteria smelled exactly like my last one: peanut butter, disinfectant, and mystery meat. Lunch trays clattered and kids gabbed. My brown bag crunched in my sweaty fist. Imogene steered me over to a table near the middle where her two friends were waiting.

"You can sit here," she said, her teeth shining in my face.

I searched far and wide for an empty table where I could sit alone, like I always have, but every seat was filled. Plus, I'd never been invited to sit by anyone before, so maybe I should just go with it as part of my brand-new-me experiment? But Imogene gave me the creeps. She was like one of those really fancy dolls who come alive at night to kill you. I'd have to keep an eye on her.

"Thanks." I plopped down on the hard plastic bench. Sister Marie Francis (secret cowgirl) had packed my lunch that morning. I peeked inside and found an apple and a ham sandwich. At least it wasn't oatmeal.

The fifth-grade ambassador tossed her shiny hair over her shoulder. "Girls, this is Bernice. She just moved here from Kansas City. Bernice, these are the girls. Kristy and Heather."

I stared at both of them and they stared at me. No one spoke. No one ate. I resisted the urge to pick my nose, so progress.

"Bernice, tell us about Kansas City?" Imogene asked, her blue eyes skimming past mine.

"Well, I mean . . . I guess it's all right. I lived outside the big part of the city, though."

"Like in a suburb?" Kristy asked, sounding bored.

"More like a trailer park." I could've thrown the mic

down and walked off the stage then, 'cause all three girls stared at me, bug-eyed.

Imogene cleared her throat. "We don't have one of those here."

I took a big bite of my sandwich and chewed. "Half-way should have mobile homes. 'Cause they are halfway between a house and an RV, right?" I snorted at my own joke.

The girls smiled weakly at me and then got very interested in eating their chicken nuggets.

Imogene made a face while I licked a blob of mayonnaise off my shirt, so I stopped midlick and grabbed a napkin off Kristy's tray.

"Geez. You would think someone your size would have more experience eating," Kristy said, and they all giggled like maniacs.

Nobody at my old school would have dared to call me fat and then laugh at me. They would have known that a beatdown was coming. If not from me, then from one of my brothers. But I was all alone here, and I was trying to be somebody different. Somebody who didn't punch people on the first day of school. I took a deep breath and shrugged as another blob of mayo ended up on my jeans.

A man wearing a plaid suit jacket with those little elbow patches walked up beside our table, and Imogene's voice got all high and weird.

"I can't wait to show you all around Halfway Primary, Bernice. I promise to do whatever it takes to make you feel welcome here."

The man, who was clasping his hands behind his back, smiled tightly at Imogene.

"Oh, Principal Jenkins, I didn't see you there!" Her eyelashes blinked so fast I thought she might take flight.

"I see you've all met our new student. Pleasure to meet you, Bernice."

I nodded dumbly.

"I've attended St. Drogo's with your aunt for many years now."

"Thank you for the computer, sir. The sisters said you made sure it was ready to go."

He smiled and patted my shoulder, and I heard Imogene take a sharp breath. She grabbed my arm and said in a voice loud enough so everyone in a ten-mile radius could hear her, "Bernice, you must come to my birthday party this weekend. It's at my house, at four on Saturday." She looked at my stained KISS T-shirt and added in a whisper, "Wear something decent."

I think Heather kicked Imogene under the table, but she didn't even flinch. Principal Jenkins gave our table a nod before walking off. I might've thrown up in my mouth at her suck-up-ityness. Imogene was terrible, but I had my first-ever birthday party invitation.

10

To Party, or Not to Party?

I walked home, my backpack heavy with homework plus makeup work. The air smelled weird out here . . . like rain and hay and cow poop. The sun hung high in the sky, and I stopped by the wooden fence behind the abbey to see if I could get a glimpse of Sister Marie Francis horseback riding again. No such luck.

The rest of the school day had been confusing. Imogene and her friends were polite to my face, but I caught them giggling behind their hands a few times, and I wouldn't have been shocked if the joke was on me. Most of the other kids ignored me, and that was fine. If I wanted to stay out of trouble, it was probably better I wasn't tempted to punch anyone.

I thought about Oliver Stratts back home and wondered if he ever thought about me. I hoped he wasn't still mad about the dog poo situation.

I wondered if Momma and Lloyd had made it to

California yet, or if they'd blown all my hard-earned fake-dog-charity money on beef jerky and Mountain Dew. I wondered if my brothers missed me. Who was gonna judge their trampoline jumps while I was gone?

Luckily, I wouldn't be here forever. I'd figure out a way to earn my money, and then I'd be on a bus headed for California. Maybe I'd even stop at wherever Momma and Lloyd were staying along the way. And then I'd spend two glorious weeks at stunt camp, where I'd be good at everything and everyone would want to be my friend. I let out a long slow breath.

It was dead quiet inside the abbey, and I let a loud burp rip to break up the silence. It bounced off the beige walls of the basement living quarters, but no one came to investigate. I shuffled past the plaid couch and the kitchen table, and finally ended up in my own room.

I threw my backpack on the quilt and sat down in front of the computer. I felt homesick, but I wasn't even sure why. It's not like Momma was always home when I got back from school. But at least the TV would've blared and one of my brothers would've put me in a headlock. It was the loud kind of quiet around here.

Thoughts of Imogene's birthday bounced around in my head and I, once again, told myself there was no way I was gonna show up.

But I was invited, and I'd never gotten invited to a party before. Maybe I'd go for a little bit, to see how dorky it was. I could try out being a regular kid hanging out with all her regular friends.

Wait, it wasn't like Imogene had tried to be my friend . . . had she?

I frowned and stared at my dumb reflection in the black computer screen. This was all new territory for Bernice Buttman. I was used to kids hating me, fearing me, and avoiding me. But I had no idea how to tell if someone was actually trying to be my friend for real.

The next question was, did I even want that beastly girl to be my friend? She kissed up harder than a politician with a pile of babies. I wasn't confident I could resist putting gum in her hair for any amount of time.

I fired up the computer and plucked the green notebook from my backpack. I didn't have very much to research today, but I'd written down one question:

How can I raise money for camp?

I clicked away and Google provided me with some helpful ideas, which all involved selling things. That seemed hard when I didn't have any friends or family to sell to.

I clicked onto my email account and started a new letter to Ms. Knightley.

Dear Ms. Knightley,

I bet you miss me there at the library! You probably haven't touched any gum or wiped orange cheese ball powder off anything for days.

My new situation is . . . Well, I don't know what it is yet. I wanted to hate it here, but the nuns are really nice and I have my own room and my own computer. School is school. It would stink no matter where I went.

Sister Angela-Clarence has been around since dirt was new and only talks in book quotes. You two would get along like beans and weenies.

I got invited to a birthday party, but I don't think I'll go because I'm sure the girl only asked to be nice. Or maybe she asked to be mean. It's really confusing. Besides, I've never gone to a party before and I wouldn't know what to do.

Your friend,
Bernice Buttman

I'd only read a few sentences in *The Hobbit* (my homework) when my email dinged with Ms. Knightley's reply.

Dear Bernice,

I'm so glad to hear from you. The library is terribly dull without my best researcher. I'm glad you're settling in and getting your footing in your new life.

Remember you're a smart, funny girl. If someone invited you to a birthday party, it was because they knew you would add to the enjoyment of the day. And they would be right.

I want to hear all about this event after you go.

Your friend,
Ms. Knightley

Well, that settled it, then. I guess I was gonna go to my first nonfamily birthday shindig. But I wouldn't bet any of my camp money on me adding enjoyment to anyone's day.

• • • •

Saturday morning I washed my hair and yanked it into two tight pigtails on either side of my head. If possible, it made my cheeks look even fatter. I looked exactly like Momma.

I stuck my tongue out at my reflection in the mirror and yanked the pigs back out. I would let my hair be wild and free, which was much more Bernice than Momma.

I found a WWF T-shirt that wasn't too rumply or smelly, and *boom*, I was ready for a birthday party. All I needed was a present. Part of me wanted to get Imogene something really terrible. I imagined myself wrapping up one of the abbey's hymnals, or maybe a steaming pile of horse doo from the pasture. That would serve her right for confusing me about parties.

But on the other hand, it wouldn't hurt to get her something more impressive. What did fifth-grade girls get each other for their birthdays? I had no idea. My aunt had pressed a ten-dollar bill in my hand as soon as she heard about the party, and I was sorely tempted to add it to my camp fund and forget this whole business. Except I'd never gone to a party before and I'd heard they had cake.

I decided to go walk around Halfway and see if I got any ideas. The courthouse stood in the middle of the square, an American flag flying high from its tallest peak. Tiny shops with colorful awnings and hand-painted signs lined the outer streets.

An old-fashioned ice cream parlor's sign read ONLY DRIVE-THROUGH IN TOWN! A guy on a horse ordered at the window. That was something you didn't see in Kansas City!

Back home, when it was my birthday (June tenth), my family celebrated with burgers and dogs on the grill.

Momma stacked unwrapped Twinkies like Lincoln Logs and stuck candles in the top layer for my cake. My brothers sang the "you look like a monkey" version of the birthday song. And my uncle Earl . . .

Dang! I had a brilliant idea about what to get Imogene for her present. A little bit of the Lone Star Trailer Park all wrapped up and tied with a bow. I grinned to myself, and then went in the general store to find all the supplies I needed.

The whole rest of the morning I was busier than a one-legged cat in a sandbox.

• • • •

Four o'clock came, and my aunt offered to drive me to the party in the clunky old church van. I only agreed because I had absolutely no idea where Imogene lived.

"Are you excited?" Aunt Josephine asked.

"I guess so." I watched the neat yards of Halfway fly by my window.

My aunt cleared her throat. "I hope I don't have to tell you to be on your best behavior. Imogene's father is the mayor of Halfway."

I surely did not care what kind of an impression I made on a stuffy old mayor, but just then we rounded a corner and pulled into the circle drive of a huge white house. It had tall columns on either side of the porch and a balcony over the front door. It was big, and there were no wheels under it, that was for sure. I felt my mouth fill up with too much spit.

"Have a great time, Bernice."

I clamped my lips shut as I got out of the van, lugging my squashy present and slamming the door behind me. The shadow of the house swallowed me up, and I stood frozen on the sidewalk, wondering if I should ring the bell.

My aunt backed the rusty van onto the street as another car pulled in. Kristy from Mr. Newton's class came out of a black SUV, fluffing her hair. She breezed past me, carrying her package toward the backyard, and I decided to follow.

When I cleared the corner of the house I let out a low whistle. Round tables decorated the green grass, draped with cotton-candy-pink tablecloths and shaded by pink umbrellas. Crystal chandeliers dripped from the umbrella supports, and fancy china plates sparkled in the sunshine. It looked like someone had upchucked a bottle of Pepto. A real live band played music, but it weren't no Lynyrd Skynyrd—just some ol' violins and that sorta thing.

I spied the birthday girl greeting her guests as they placed their fancy gifts on a long white table. I marched on over and gave her my best smile.

"Hello, Imogene. Happy birthday." I thrust the package into her hands.

She smiled weakly and put the present down without looking at it too close. "Oh, Bernice. I didn't think you'd come."

I swallowed. "You invited me."

"Yes, of course. I thought for sure you'd have more important things to do on a Saturday than hang out with a bunch of kids you don't even know."

"Not really." I crossed my arms and we had a staring contest. I concentrated on shooting laser beams out my eyes to melt her head into a blob of goo.

Kristy stepped up to us and waved her hand in front of my face, but I refused to blink. Imogene finally looked away and I smiled like a jack-o'-lantern.

"Did the St. Drogo's van drop you off?" Kristy asked.

"Yeah, so?"

"Why? It isn't even Sunday."

"I live at St. Drogo's. With my aunt."

The happy hostess smirked. "You *live* in a church? Doesn't the holy stuff start sizzling when you walk by?" She laughed hysterically at her own joke.

A part of me wanted to jab her in the ribs and skip back to the abbey, but I decided to try another tactic.

"It's not so bad. I can eat all the Communion wafers I want, so that's pretty sweet."

The two girls looked at me like I'd said I ate puppies for breakfast, so I escaped to the snack table to let them scrape their jaws off the floor.

There were no good eats over there. A few kids smeared dry crackers with black gunk, and I poked a lump of runny cheese with the tiny knife meant to cut it. "Good gravy!

This girl's got more money than the Monopoly man. You'd think she'd be able to afford some decent snacks."

One of the girls, a redhead I recognized from school, giggled behind her hand. "It's caviar," she whispered as I plopped a tiny spoonful of black gunk on my plate.

"You don't say," I mumbled.

The redhead giggled some more. "I'm Francie."

"Bernice," I said, taking a few teeny-tiny ears of corn for my plate. "And if this is what people eat at birthday parties, count me out."

"Imogene likes to show off," Francie said. "None of us like eating this stuff. Except for the cake, of course."

She nodded to a tower of white-and-pink frosting displayed on its own table. Well, paint me green and call me a cucumber. That was more like it.

"The rest of her parties are always terrible, but the cake is to die for."

I gave Francie a small smile. All that giggling made her seem a few fries short of a Happy Meal, but at least she didn't eat fish eggs for fun. For the first time since twinkly-eyed Oliver, I was thinking someone had friend potential.

"Can I tell you a secret?" I whispered. She leaned in a bit. "I'm so nervous I don't know whether to scratch my watch or wind my butt."

Francie smiled at me. She had a gap between her big front teeth. "Bernice, you aren't even wearing a watch!"

11

Fun and Games

Some fat guy in a suit clanked a crystal glass like you see 'em do in the movies and announced it was time for Imogene to open her presents. She draped her puffy pink dress over a chair set up in front of the gift table, and a real live maid in a uniform handed her presents one by one. She got lots of jewelry, a few books, and a bunch of gift cards. After opening each item she smiled tightly and thanked the person who gave it to her. Real fine manners, but her words needed sweetness, that's for sure.

She held up a Barbie in a shiny pink dress (the two of them looked like Twinkies!) and told Francie, "Thanks for the *doll*. My little sister has this same one." Francie's cheeks turned redder than a baboon's butt and I felt my fists clench tight.

My lumpy present was the only one left on the table.

The maid pinched it between two fingers and set it in Imogene's lap like it was a dirty diaper.

"There isn't a card on this, but I'm going to guess from the wrap job it's from Bernice," Imogene said, smirking.

"It's what's inside that counts!" I said. My fingers ticked against my leg and I was nercited for her to open it. (Nercited = nervous + excited.)

She peeled back the brown paper bag I'd tied with a red ribbon and pulled out my creation.

"What. Is. This?" The birthday girl forgot to put on her syrupy-sweet voice.

"It's a piñata! My uncle Earl makes them for all my birthdays."

"What's it supposed to be shaped like?" She held it up and let it spin on its string.

"It's a horse." I could admit, it was only loosely horse-shaped. "Tie it to a tree and let's have a whack!"

Imogene sniffed at the lumpy blue horse, but everyone else clapped and cheered, so she slung on her toothy smile and asked the maid to string it up.

The kids took turns wearing the mayor's tie around their eyes and swinging a golf club at the bouncing blue horse. I held my breath, waiting for the moment when his butt would fall off.

After everyone else had tried, Francie shoved the club in my hands and wrapped my eyes with the expensive-smelling tie. This was gonna be my chance to win the game and a partyful of friends.

I wound up and swung my hardest.

I felt the club connect with the papery horse and heard the tear that meant he'd split.

I heard the kids screaming and scrambling.

And then I heard dead silence.

I whipped off the blindfold with a tongue-out grin, like Farkle the fake dog, and looked around at the stunned party people. "Did I get 'em? Why aren't you chewing?"

"There's no candy in there!" someone shouted.

"These are cheese balls! Who puts cheese balls in a piñata?"

"Look at the cake!"

Everyone gasped when they noticed the four-tiered cake covered with fluorescent-orange balls.

Uh-oh. Things were not going to plan. "I think it looks better," I mumbled.

"Is this some kind of joke?" Imogene crossed her twiggy arms and scowled at me.

So much for making a partyful of friends! Imogene thought I was trying to sabotage her special day.

I tried to explain. "We always put cheese balls in our piñatas. I thought it'd be fun."

"And did you think it would be fun to *ruin* my party, after I was nice enough to invite you?"

My eyes bumped from guest to guest, all of them staring at me with open mouths.

"I thought I could add to the enjoyment of your day," I said quietly.

Everyone gawked at me, and not one of them smiled.

Imogene sniffed. "Nobody wants you here, Buttman. Nobody in this whole entire town." The mayor put a protective arm around his daughter, but not before Imogene's voice had sunk into my guts. I felt the truth in her words. *Nobody wants me here.* For once all the fight-back had left my body, and all I wanted was to get out of there pronto.

I started the long hike back to the abbey before I even got a bite of that delicious cheese ball cake.

• • • •

The nuns popped out of their kitchen chairs when I dragged my sorry behind through the back door of St. Drogo's.

"How did you get home? The party isn't over for another hour."

"Weren't we supposed to come get you?"

"How was it? Were there fancy cheeses?"

The only one who didn't grill me was the wrinkly Sister Angela-Clarence. I guess she didn't have a book quote about birthday disasters.

I halfheartedly answered their questions and then escaped to my room. It had all been going all right, and then I'd gone and flubbed it up. My first-ever party invitation had gone as well as a pogo stick competition in quicksand.

I pulled some cheese balls out of my pocket and crunched angrily.

Stupid birthdays.

Stupid Imogene.

Stupid me.

I plopped into my desk chair and pulled up my email, punching the keys maybe a little too hard. I huffed and snorted as my fingers flew across the letters.

Dear Ms. Knightley,

The party was a disaster and all those kids hate me and this whole town hates me and I am mad that you even told me to go.

Done and Dusted,
Bernice Buttman

There was a quiet knock on my door, and Sister Marie Francis let herself in. I expected her to gab on about the mayor's house, but she sat on the edge of my bed instead.

"Bernice, I wonder if you could help me with something."

"What?" I mumbled, my eyes glued to the desk.

"I need help with the horses. I'm getting older now, and they're a lot of work. If you'd do some of the grooming and cleaning, I'd give you riding lessons. Would you like that?"

Horseback riding was a skill every stuntwoman needed.

The thought lifted me up like helium balloons tied to my underwear.

"Yeah. I think I could do that!" My fingers itched to Google everything about stunt riding as soon as Marie Francis left.

"Wonderful. You'll start tomorrow. Oh, and this is from Sister Angela-Clarence." She handed me a folded-up square of paper and walked out the door.

The handwriting was small and cramped, and I had to squint to make out the words:

> *"Isn't it nice to think that tomorrow is a new day with no mistakes in it yet?"*
>
> *–L. M. Montgomery, Anne of Green Gables*

Tomorrow.

Everything would be better tomorrow.

12

Cowgirl Up

Sunday was church, and I sat dutifully in my pew, counting the rafters and trying not to scratch myself. The nuns sat in a row by themselves, and an ancient-looking priest yammered on about something I didn't understand. Time seemed to stand still, but finally he gave the ten other churchgoers and me a blessing and we tasted freedom.

I tried not to be impatient as Sister Marie Francis talked to each and every person filing out of the church, but I finally caught her eye. She smiled at me and I mimed riding a horse. Well, it started out as a mime, but I let a "Yee-haw" slip out, turning a few heads. She smiled and nodded. I was ready for my first riding lesson.

You know how some people have a real natural connection with animals? Well, that ain't me. The only kind of pets we've ever had were big old hound dogs sniffin' around under our porch. Oh, and a raccoon snuck under there from time to time. But standing nose to nose with an eleven-hundred-pound horse (I'd Googled it) made my stomach twist like two cats fighting in a burlap sack.

The inside of the barn smelled musty, and there was the definite twang of dookie mixed with hay. The autumn light slid through the cracks in the wood-plank walls and picked up shimmery dust floating in the air.

The giant beast in front of me was the color of butterscotch and he had blond hair like me. Actually, his looked nicer than mine, so I'm glad it wasn't a beauty contest. Mary-Francis called him a palomino.

"That's a dumb name. Pal-o-mean-o."

"No, palomino is his breed. His name is Hoof. Last name Hearted."

"Hoof Hearted." As soon as I said it out loud, I cracked up. I had a feeling me and Hoof Hearted would get along just fine.

Sister Mary-Francis hummed as she showed me how to use a spiky oval currycomb to knock the crust off Hoof's coat and then use the stiff brush to get the rest. She demonstrated how to brush his tail and clean out the hooves (which kind of scared me because what if he didn't enjoy having his feet messed with? If you touched any of my piggies it was grounds for a roundhouse kick to the face!). Finally Mary-Francis had my destiny all saddled up.

"Have you ridden a horse before, Bernice?"

"Only the one that takes quarters outside the Walmart."

"This will be pretty similar. Ready to try?"

My eyes trailed nervously up Hoof's long neck. His ears were plastered flat back against his head. Maybe he'd heard the sister compare him to the Walmart horse? Maybe he was trying to calculate how much I weighed? Either way, he did not look happy about the situation.

I swallowed hard. "Sure. Let's go."

Sister Marie Francis eyed my green Crocs. "No self-respecting cowgirl would wear those in the barn. Here."

She handed me a beat-up pair of tennis shoes that were not even a little bit less ugly, and I tied them on. I climbed up in the stirrup (always from the left side!) and I gave Hoof a withering glance before swinging my weight onto the saddle. *Lights, camera, action.*

Hoof gave a mighty snort.

He jerked the lead rope right out of Sister Marie Francis's hands.

He took off running like the devil himself was chasing us.

We streaked out of the barn before Sister Marie Francis even knew what had happened. I grabbed a handful of mane and gripped the saddle horn with white knuckles. I jiggled more than the preschoolers did when my brothers took over the bounce house.

The pasture blurred by and I didn't even have reins to try and steer. I yelled every horse word I'd ever heard.

"Whoa!"

"Ho!"

"Whoa, Nelly!"

"STOP!"

"Brakes!"

But Hoof Hearted ran like his butt was on fire.

I felt my grip loosening. I didn't know how much longer I'd be able to hold on. And in the distance I saw the wooden fence at the end of the field.

"Turn around! There's a fence up there!" *Oh no, oh no, oh no!* He wasn't going to try and jump the fence, was he? I didn't think I was ready for advanced stunt work on my very first lesson.

That dang horse didn't slow down. If anything, he picked up speed. I could hear Marie Francis yelling from behind us, but she sounded a long ways off.

The fence got closer and closer and I tried the only other thing I'd seen cowboys do in the movies.

I kicked Hoof Hearted hard in the ribs.

And he skidded to a stop and ducked his head.

And I rolled over his neck and landed in a big old pile of yesterday's oats.

I lay there, looking at the puffy white clouds in the sky, seriously reconsidering my stunt camp plans. All the air had gone out of me, and I was pretty sure I would hurt everywhere when I stood up.

Sister Marie Francis trotted over and hovered above me.

"Are you all right? I have no idea what came over Hoof. He's usually so gentle!" She was out of breath, her face red.

The devil-horse snorted and stomped his foot.

A real stuntwoman wouldn't be afraid of some dumb horse. A real stuntwoman gets deep purple bruises every day at work, exactly like the ones blooming on my backside. A real stuntwoman could've repeated that fool dismount until they got the right shot.

I crossed my arms and squinted my eyes at him.

"We aren't done here, horse. Fact, we haven't even begun."

Hoof shook his head like he was shaking off flies, but I swear his lips stretched across his teeth in a smile.

13

Squeezy Cheese

The first Saturday in October brought a fresh breeze that stirred the still-green leaves and promised crisper fall weather soon.

I sat at my computer, my pillow shoved under my rump. My backside still hurt like whoa, but the rest of my bruises had faded a bit from last weekend's horseback disaster.

My email icon blinked at me, and I clicked it to find a new message from Ms. Knightley. My finger hesitated on the mouse, remembering the email I'd sent to her after the party, but curiosity won out, and I braced myself for whatever she could say.

Dear Bernice,

I'm so sorry to hear you didn't enjoy the birthday party, but I am proud of you for going. It takes guts to try something new, and making friends is one of the most difficult challenges in life. I've always known you were a brave girl, and you prove it to me each time you put yourself out there. Keep trying and don't ever give up.

Your friend,
Ms. Knightley

Well, that made me feel about as tall as a worm stretched sideways.

Leave it to Ms. Knightley to call me brave when I felt like a big ol' doofus. The last week at school had been brutal. Imogene had gone around telling everyone who wasn't already there how I'd ruined her party. It seemed like the whole school, and maybe even the whole town, was on the Bernice-is-the-worst bandwagon. I tried to keep my head down and ignore everyone, but the Old Bernice wanted to punch Imogene in the cherry-lip-glossed mouth.

I took a deep breath and stretched, feeling the week-old bruises complain. My stomach rumbled, and I decided it was time to head to the kitchen for lunch.

Aunt Josephine had left a note on the table about the nuns going to do some work in the community. She'd also left me five dollars to go get lunch. *Score.*

I was still sore, but the more I walked toward the town square, the better I felt.

The five dollars was burning a hole in my pocket. The plan was to get a can of squeezy cheese and a box of crackers for around two-fifty at the general store, and that left me another two-fifty for my stunt camp fund. Just two thousand four hundred ninety-four dollars and fifty cents left to go.

I pushed the door of the general store and the tinkling bells announced my arrival. The aisles were bright and neatly organized, and a few Saturday shoppers meandered down the rows. I headed for the cracker aisle and had pulled a box off the shelf when a familiar voice froze me to the spot.

"Oh, Mr. Jenkins! How wonderful to see you here."

"Hello, Imogene." The principal sounded tired.

"How's your family?"

"Oh, just fine."

"Wonderful."

Somebody whispered directly in my ear, and I dropped my box of Wheaty-Wows.

"That girl sucks up more than a vacuum salesman."

I spun around and was face to face with Francie, the redheaded girl from the birthday party.

"Oh, hey." I stretched my neck to see if I could spy my nemesis through the canned goods. "Who cares about sucking up to the principal on a Saturday? What's the point?" I was mostly talking to myself, but Francie answered anyway.

"She never takes a break. She'd bring muffin baskets to

his house once a week if she thought it would help her get the Principal's Citizenship Award."

I peered through a crack between two cans and watched Imogene yammer on. Our poor principal looked like a squirrel trying to cross a road.

"What's the Principal's Citizenship Award?" I whispered. The last thing I wanted to do was get that horrible girl's attention after the birthday party disaster. She mentioned a "Yippee Pie Yay Festival" to Mr. Jenkins and I shook my head to clear those ridiculous words out.

"It's this award they give out to one fifth-grade kid each year. If you win you get a thousand dollars and a trip to Jefferson City to meet the governor."

A thousand bucks would get me a lot closer to stunt camp. But Bernice Buttman was not the kind of girl who won citizenship awards. I was the kind of girl who kicked those prizewinners in the shins. *Oh, well.*

"That explains why she's always fake-nice to me when Jenkins is around," I muttered.

"She's the worst."

"Why does she even want a dumb award? She doesn't need the money. She's using dollar bills to wipe her tush up in her mansion. And her dad's the mayor! I bet she could go meet the governor any ol' time she wants."

Francie shrugged. "My mom says some people are never satisfied."

And then a lightbulb turned on in my brain. Or maybe

it was a Check Engine light. But either way, I knew exactly what to do. I picked up the Wheaty-Wows and shoved them into Francie's hands, then walked around the aisle to where Imogene and Mr. Jenkins were chatting.

I wormed right into the conversation. "Hey, how's everybody today?"

"Just fine. Actually, I must get going." Mr. Jenkins clutched his loaf of bread with an iron grip. He backed away from the two of us like we were gonna steal his wallet and run.

"What are *you* doing here?" Imogene hissed.

"Buying some stuff to take to the food bank that the nuns run," I said, a little too loudly. "I live at St. Drogo's with the nuns, remember, Mr. Jenkins?"

"Yes. Sister Marie Francis says you've been quite the blessing to them. And how wonderful that you've taken an interest in helping the poor."

"I consider myself a global *citizen*, sir. Always looking out for others."

Mr. Jenkins nodded thoughtfully, and I smiled at Imogene as he walked away.

"Leave me alone," she growled through clenched-up teeth.

"Sure thing," I said. "Just thought I'd let the principal know what a good *citizen* I am."

"If you're talking about getting the Principal's Citizenship Award, you can forget it. I've been volunteering after school for years to prove to everyone how good a citizen I am. Living with nuns doesn't make you good."

"I'm sure you're right. And I don't care if I win any dumb awards. But it sure would make me happy if *you* didn't."

Imogene's eye twitched, and she might've yelled at me right there in the general store, but Mr. Jenkins hurried by with his bread in a bag, and she had to clench her jaw shut. I smiled real big again and went to retrieve my crackers from Francie.

"That. Was. Awesome," she said as I rounded the corner. "Nobody ever talks to Imogene like that."

"I talk to everyone like that."

Francie rubbed her freckled nose. "Hey, you probably don't want to, but I got squeezy cheese, and you've got crackers. We could take 'em to the park and share?"

That would put another dollar fifty in my bank account. Plus, it's not like I had anything better to do, so I agreed.

She put her skinny little arm around me as we walked out the door, and I wondered if I'd managed to get myself a friend without even writing a ransom note.

• • • •

My whole body hurt after me and Hoof faced off the following Monday, and Aunt Josephine's eyebrows crashed together when I limped through the kitchen to pour my cereal.

"Maybe you should take a break from your riding lessons," she said, pouring some orange juice in a glass for me. "I promised my sister I'd return you in one piece."

I snorted at the mention of Momma. *As if she'd care how many pieces I was in.* Chucknorris had sent me a postcard last week, and from what I could tell (he couldn't spell worth a lick), Momma had taken up jazz dancing because she thought it would beef up her résumé, and she hadn't bothered to check in on little old me.

"You'll most likely get worse before you get better," Sister Marie Francis said, nodding at me.

Sister Angela-Clarence hummed softly and sipped her tea. At first, I didn't think she even knew what we were talking about, but then she said, "*Oh! If people knew what a comfort to a horse a light hand is . . .*"

Aunt Josephine interpreted my confused look. "It's from *Black Beauty.*"

"Well, it's not Hoof who needs the gentle hand," I said, rubbing my backside.

"A break, then?" Marie Francis asked, eyebrows raised.

"Seriously, it's not too bad," I told them, although it actually was pretty bad. But I didn't want to quit my riding lessons. I hadn't learned any cool stunts yet.

Aunt Josephine drove me to school in the St. Drogo's van, and I felt my heart do a flip in my chest when I saw the kids streaming in the front door. Did they all hate me? Did this entire town hate me? Who was I here? I knew myself about as good as these creepy kids knew me—which was not at all.

My aunt put her hand on my knee and gave it a squeeze. "Stay out of trouble, Bernice."

I tried to look offended, but my triple-chin smirk broke into a smile. "Who, me? I wouldn't know trouble from nothing."

She gave me a squint-eyed stare and practically pushed me out the door.

I dragged my feet all the way to the fifth-grade pod. But the first face I saw when I pushed through the door was a friendly one.

"Hey, Bernice! I asked Mr. Newton if we could sit by each other and he said he didn't care. So now we're desk buddies!" Francie's cheeks pinked up with excitement, and her red curls seemed extra springy.

Desk buddies? I was starting to regret sharing squeezy cheese with this girl. Bernice Buttman wasn't anyone's desk buddy.

At least I never had been before. Old Bernice wasn't anyone's buddy, but maybe New Bernice could be?

If Francie wasn't tricking, she might be the only kid in this whole town who cared two hoots about me. My insides twisted up at the thought of being someone's real actual friend. It was what I'd always wanted, but I had no idea how to do it.

Maybe I could treat this whole being nice thing like it

was a part I'd been assigned. Like acting. Yeah. I was the stunt double for the nicest girl in school, so I had to follow her around and do everything she did. And if she ended up jumping off the building or something, that would be my part, of course.

I let out a breath. *Be nice.* It was harder than it sounded. I gave Francie a cringing smile and headed over to our buddy desks.

Mr. Newton might have been in the mood to grant Francie a desk buddy, but he scowled at me as I took my seat, and I swallowed hard.

Right out of the gate, he was like a dog with a new bone. He called on me three times during the discussion of *The Hobbit*, and even though I'd read it I couldn't get my mouth to shake hands with my brain and spit smart-ish words out. His mustache twitched, and he reached for his sanitizer to wash away the stupid germs I was spreading in his classroom.

Then it was time for math, and again I was completely lost. The problems all looked like chicken scratches up there on the whiteboard. Mr. Newton asked me to go up and solve a real doozy. We both let out a heavy sigh as I stared at the problem for several long minutes, only to write a huge question mark after the equals sign and march back to my desk. Most of the kids laughed, and not in a polite way.

The hand sanitizer came out again.

I was so relieved when it was time for lunch. I needed a break from being the class dunce. But as I stood up, prepared to face a cafeteria full of Imogene's bad attitude, Mr. Newton asked me to stay after class. Francie gave me a worried look and whispered, "I'll save you a spot."

The students filed out of the classroom until it was just me and the tyrant of the fifth grade.

I stared at a poster of tall mountains and white puffy clouds that read *I left my heart in Middle Earth.* If there was any way to teleport yourself into a poster, I'd have paid my entire stunt camp fund to learn how just then.

"Bernice. I'm sure I don't have to tell you, you're behind here."

I nodded, staring at Middle Earth.

"I don't see you applying yourself to catch up."

I clenched my teeth and wrenched my eyes away from the poster to stare at my lap. "I'm trying, sir. It's only been a month. I've done all the work you assigned."

"Your class participation today would prove otherwise."

I dug my fingernails into my palms. "I don't want to talk in front of the other kids."

He leaned back in his chair and reached for that dang hand sanitizer. I itched to write *long-term effects of alcohol sanitizer on bacteria* in my green notebook. He was probably causing a supervirus.

"Mr. Newton? You have a phone call in the office." The

voice on the intercom sounded bored, but Mr. Newton shot out of his chair like it was Gandalf the Great waiting on line one.

"We'll discuss this in depth later," he said, dashing out of the room.

I sat there staring at the bottle of hand sanitizer and feeling bubbles of anger boil out of my ears.

I don't care much about being called fat or ugly. Those are just other people's two-cent opinions. But I get a real bee in my bonnet when people call me stupid. Momma likes to tell people I was off vandalizin' on the day God passed out brains. And people are always telling me I'll never amount to nothing, like the rest of the Buttmans. They're all so sure I'll turn out just like Momma. My nostrils flared remembering all those times people said I had rocks for brains.

Kids at my old school.

Momma.

Mr. Newton.

And then, like a present from Gandalf himself, I noticed the bottle of glue sitting smack-dab in the middle of Mr. Newton's desk. Right next to the hand sanitizer.

It was the clear kind of glue. It was the clear kind of sanitizer. And my hands had taken action before my brain had a chance to catch up. It was just too easy. Even for a dummy like me.

A few seconds later I had completed my task, and I

hurried out to the cafeteria to scarf down whatever Sister Marie Francis had packed for my lunch. But I couldn't stop smiling. It was like I'd greased my teeth with Vaseline.

I counted down the minutes until Mr. Newton started feeling germy again.

So much for nice. Nice was overrated.

It was perfect, like something out of a movie. After lunch Mr. Newton asked me a question, which once again I had no answer for. His face clouded over and his mustache twitched. He reached for his hand sanitizer and put a large plop on his palm. He started to rub his hands together, all while still scowling at me.

I tried hard to keep my face completely blank, but *dang*, it was hard with the glue making little boogers all over his hands. He kept rubbing and rubbing them, getting more and more frustrated. His face turned the color of old hamburger. The kids finally caught on to the fact that the sanitizer had been compromised, and so it was finally okay for me to laugh along with the rest of them. But my teacher was not laughing.

14

Yippie Pie Yay

Mr. Newton's glue hands were all anyone could talk about. Well, that and the Yippie Pie Yay Festival, which was coming up in a few days. Why a bunch of elementary school kids would get so worked up over a pie carnival had me scratching my head.

"So what's the deal with this festival?" I asked Sister Marie Francis while we walked back to the abbey after my riding lesson. I'd managed to stay on Hoof Hearted for the whole thing, so I considered it a pretty big success. I'd be riding upside down in no time.

"The Yippie Pie Yay Festival has been a time-honored Halfway tradition since the early nineteen hundreds."

"Do we have to call it that?" I asked, plucking the heads off some wheat. Or maybe weeds. I wasn't one hundred percent sure.

Sister Marie Francis looked at me sideways. "That's what it's called."

I scrunched up my face. "Cornier than Kansas in August."

She patted me on the shoulder. "It's fun! Everyone in town bakes pies and brings them to the town square. On Friday there's a carnival with games and rides. Then on Saturday night there's a dance and pie contests."

"Like ribbons for the best-tasting pie? Or pie-eating contests?"

The sister raised her eyebrows. "Both."

We pushed open the back door to the abbey, which spilled into the tiny kitchen. My aunt Josephine and Sister Angela-Clarence sat at the small kitchen table.

"Bernice and I were discussing the Yippie Pie Yay Festival," Marie Francis said.

I plopped onto one of the hard wooden chairs. "Do we *have* to call it that?"

"That's what it's called," Aunt Josephine said. "Now, what kind of pie did you plan on bringing to the festival?"

Sister Angela-Clarence sat bolt straight all of a sudden and yelled, "*He was put in a pie by Mrs. McGregor!*"

My aunt rubbed the confused old lady on the arm. "Hush, now, Sister. Nobody is getting baked into a pie. That's Peter Rabbit's father you're thinking of."

I bit my lip to try to keep from laughing, but also because I was thinking hard about pies. There was only one kind of pie my momma ever made.

"How 'bout some PB and J Pinchy Pies?"

I got blank stares from the sisters, so I explained to them the magic of the Pinchy Pie.

"You take two slices of Wonder Bread and make a peanut butter and jelly sandwich out of 'em. Then you use a cup to cut it out in the shape of a circle."

My aunt interrupted. "I think what you are describing is called a *sandwich*, Bernice. Not a pie."

I glared at her. "I wasn't done. Then you use your fingers to pinch around the edges of the sandwich and *then* you deep fry it in Crisco." I made the sound of the sizzling grease. "It makes like little hand pies and they are sooo dang delicious."

Aunt Josephine's voice softened. "This festival is a big deal, Bernice. It might be a good way to show the town you're one of them."

"By making a pie?" I gave her the openmouthed stink eye.

"By making an amazing pie," she said.

"So you're telling me if I somehow manage to make a delicious pie for the Giddyup Cow Pie Festival everyone will like me and want to be my friend?"

"Sister Angela-Clarence got a marriage proposal one year, her lemon meringue was so good. People take this thing seriously."

The quiet old lady nodded, a huge smile on her face.

I let out a noisy huff.

"I'm not sure I even *want* everyone to like me here.

I don't need a bunch of friends calling me all the time and wanting to hang out and stuff. I got plans. Goals to work on."

The nuns looked at me with big question marks hanging over their heads. I hadn't exactly told them about my stunt camp fund yet.

"I'm sure having a few friends wouldn't be too much of a hassle," Sister Marie Francis said.

I shrugged and went to my room to Google pie recipes.

Do you know there are more than twenty million results when you type in "pie recipes" on Google? That's a lot of pie.

How was a noncooking girl like me 'sposed to know which of those recipes would win me the respect and friendship of all the nose-pickers at Halfway Primary School who currently liked me about as much as a chicken pox on the first day of summer? Which recipe would the "nicest girl at school" choose?

I put my head down on the desk and closed my eyes. Ever since Imogene's birthday, when she'd said nobody wanted me in Halfway, I'd been looking for signs that she was wrong, but they didn't amount to a hill of beans. Even after two months on my best behavior, I'd still managed to make everyone hate me.

Everyone except Francie. One friend wouldn't be so bad. Francie wasn't so bad. I only needed to come up with a pie that wouldn't un-friend Francie, and the rest of this town could pucker up and kiss my Pinchy Pies.

I sat up quick as a hot knife through butter, 'cause I had a great idea.

• • • •

I'd decided on peach pie, with an added Bernice Butt-man kick. Peach pie seemed the easiest. You didn't have to squeeze a pile of lemons or whip meringue. Laziness won out, I guess you'd say.

The nuns gave me twenty bucks the next Friday, to go get my pie-making supplies. I vowed I wouldn't spend over ten, so the rest could go in my stunt camp fund. If I kept saving at this rate, I could go to stunt camp when I was seventy. I'd be the first granny they fired out of a cannon.

I walked around the Piggly Wiggly and bought the store brand of the items on my list. Flour, sugar, lard, salt. Peaches, cornstarch, nutmeg, cinnamon.

Nutmeg was almost four dollars! I put it back. My pie would be nutmeg-less.

And then I found the secret ingredient that would make my pie the most unforgettable pie of the silly festival.

Laxi-Fast. Extra-strength. A tasteless laxative powder, sure to give all those Halfway haters the poops. Everyone from school and from this whole town who didn't want me here would soon get a bite of the Bernice Buttman Special. And the best part was, they would eat so many different pies there was no way they'd trace it back to me. It was the perfect golden flaky crime.

• • • •

The abbey was quiet when I got home, so I turned on the small transistor radio next to the stove. Someone droned on about the second coming, so I switched the station to some classic rock.

Then I dropped the bag of flour on the floor and it basically exploded.

I clenched my fists at my sides.

"If stupid could fly, I'd be a jet," I mumbled. Just like Momma always said. I scooped as much powder as I could back into the shredded bag and wiped my hands on my jeans.

With the printed recipe leading the way, I measured flour, water, salt, sugar, and lard. *Sure don't look like pie so far.* Next I was supposed to give it a whirl in a food processor. But after searching through the few kitchen cabinets, I was pretty sure the nuns didn't have one. I'd have to do this the old-fashioned way.

I hitched up my pants, then sunk both hands into the bowl, squeezing the ingredients together like clay. I giggled as the goo squished through my fingers, but a lot of the flour escaped the bowl, and by the time I was done a layer of flour-snow covered the kitchen.

My lumpy dough rolled out fine on the floor. (Well, the recipe said to roll it out on a floured surface, and I wasn't gonna dump more flour on the counter!)

When I had a big circle of dough, I spread it in the bottom of a pie pan and used a small knife to cut the extra off the edges. *Hot dang, a real pie!*

Next came the filling. I had to cut up the peaches and remove the pits. I sucked the sweet off 'em, one by one, before tossing them in the trash. I was 'sposed to peel them, too, but since I had no idea how to do that, I just skipped that step. A cup of sugar went on top, along with some lemon juice, cinnamon, and . . . nutmeg.

I didn't have nutmeg.

I poked around the spice rack and smelled a few spices before deciding on ground allspice. If it had all the spices in it, it probably had some nutmeg in there somewhere, right?

It was finally time for my secret ingredient. I carefully measured out a tablespoon of the Laxi-Fast. It said to use sparingly. But since the pie would be shared by at least eight different people, I decided to add eight tablespoons of the powder. Well, only a tiny bit was left in the bottle, so I shrugged and mixed the rest in. It made the concoction super-thick but didn't change the color too much. I smiled to myself as I licked the spoon . . . and then ran to the sink to spit it out.

I plopped my peachy filling into the waiting crust and used the scraps of dough to fashion a messy-looking criss-cross for the top. My shoes slipped across the powdery tile as I put my creation in the preheated oven and set the timer.

Whew.

Whoever made up the words *easy as pie* musta been talking about the eating of the pie, not the baking of it.

While the clock ticked and the pie made the abbey smell heavenly, I added the leftover money to my coffee can bank account. I hadn't been able to stick to my ten-dollar limit at the Piggly Wiggly. The grand total of my life's savings was now up to seven dollars and fifty-three cents. *Yee-haw.*

The timer dinged as the nuns bustled through the back door. They froze, taking in the white explosion covering the floor, the sinkful of dirty dishes, and the sticky peach sauce trailing across the counter to the stove.

"Good news," I said. "My pie's done."

Sister Marie Francis's hand fluttered to her chest, while Aunt Josephine handed me a set of pot holders. They all leaned in as I lifted my pie out of the oven. It looked good enough to eat . . . but I wouldn't advise it.

15

Bullying with a Side of Blackmail

So it occurred to me, while I was sitting there smelling delicious peach pie, that perhaps Old Bernice might have had a part in its creation. I will admit, poisoning the whole town was probably not a nice-girl move. But in my defense, most of those townspeople would chase me around with torches and pitchforks and stuff if it wasn't for the nuns. Hey, ya win some, ya lose some, right?

My pie sat on the counter, and I spent the rest of the day working on homework and waiting to deliver my creation to the festival.

The sisters had been proud of my baking, although they made me clean up the whole mess I'd made. The only thing I hated worse than cooking was cleaning, so I wasn't a big fan of this town tradition. The pie looked good, and I'd just have to make sure that pieces went fast so that the sisters, and Francie, never got a taste.

I'd just finished reading a chapter of *The Hobbit* when I

heard a knock at the abbey's kitchen door. No one but me and the nuns used that entrance, and none of us knocked. The sisters had gone out again, so I slid off my bed and headed to answer it.

Imogene stood on the porch, a bundle under one arm and a wicked smile on her face.

"What do you want?" I said, opening the door an inch and smushing my nose through the crack.

"I need to talk to you, Bernice." She grimaced at my squashed-up face. "It's important."

I narrowed my eyes but opened the door wide enough for her to come in. She glanced around the sparse room and raised one eyebrow. "This is where you live?"

I crossed my arms. "If you came here to make fun of me in my own . . . abbey, you can get out. I got things to do."

"Oh, I know you've got things to do." She patted the brown paper sack under her arm.

She was really dilling my pickle. "Get to the point."

"You're going to hand-write these thank-you cards to all the guests at my birthday party." She leaned in. "You remember my birthday party. You ruined it with your stupid cheese-ball-filled paper horse."

"My cheese-ball-ñata was the highlight of that snorefest you called a party. Make sure you write one of them thank-you notes to me."

Imogene squeezed her eyes and clenched her fists. I think she was trying to remind herself she was technically in a church. "You owe me. And if you don't do it . . . well, you'll be sorry."

I snorted. "Ooh. I'm so scared. What're you gonna do to me?"

She took a deep breath and began strolling around the kitchen. "I know something. I saw what you did."

Saw what I did? She was blowing smoke. I hadn't done anything even remotely Buttman since I got here. Except . . .

I went as white as Casper.

"That's right. You thought you were being *so sneaky*, but I went back to the classroom to get my sweater and I saw you put the glue in Mr. Newton's hand sanitizer." She stopped right in front of me and leaned in close. "You wouldn't want him to find out about that, now would you?"

Psht. "You don't have a lick of proof. It'd be my word against yours."

"Really?" she said, whipping out a fancy cell phone and holding up a picture. It featured my broad backside standing in front of Mr. Newton's desk, but even from the awkward angle, you could see the glue bottle in my hand.

I let out a long breath. It had been such a quick and easy prank, I hadn't let myself think much about it. My turning from evil to good was a work in progress! I mean, sure, I had a laxative pie cooling on the counter, but also plans to make sure it was only sampled by mean people. . . . But maybe I was doomed to live in detention and be a friendless bully? Every time I tried to turn over a new leaf, I made like a pigeon and pooped on it.

"So if I do your dumb cards, you'll get rid of that picture? You and me will be square?"

Imogene laughed. "Oh, goodness no. You'll have to do whatever I say for the rest of the school year. Now luckily, you're as dumb as you are fat, so I won't have you do any of my schoolwork. But I'm sure I can come up with *other* things for you to take care of."

Heat flashed in my belly like I'd swallowed a bunch of road flares. *Dumber than a suitcase full of doorknobs*, as Momma always said. Something inside me withered and my shoulders drooped. I yanked the crinkly package from Imogene's hands. Inside were pink note cards, pink envelopes, and shiny silver stickers.

"How'm I supposed to know what to write?"

"There's a note in the sack that lists all the gifts and givers. Use your best handwriting. I'll check them when you're finished, and if they don't look up to my standards, you can do them all again."

I threw the package down on the table and marched to the door, holding it open for Imogene. I gave her the stink eye as she bounced past me.

"Oh, and Bernice." She turned on her heels. "If they aren't done by the festival tonight, you'd better not show up. That could be a very *sticky* situation." She laughed hysterically at her own joke, exactly like a supervillain.

My knuckles were white as I gripped the knob, glaring at her stupid back as she walked away. It took all my Buttman mind power not to chase after her and slug her right in the eye. I slowly turned and winced at the pile of blackmail I had to deal with.

I'd told the nuns I'd meet them at the pie festival tonight at seven. It was already six-thirty, and the list I pulled from the bag had over two hundred names and gifts on it. *Rats!*

I paced back and forth, trying to decide what to do. Did I care if Imogene told Mr. Newton about what I'd done? I mean, it wasn't like I'd smudge a snow-white permanent record. But it would be my first offense here in Halfway. And Aunt Josephine had asked me to try and behave. Ms. Knightley wanted me to start fresh. And I wanted to try my hand at being the nice girl I hoped I could be. After the poop pie, though. Just forget about that for a minute.

I plopped down in a chair and pulled out the fat stack of cards. If I plowed through, I might still make it to the festival—a little late, but oh, well. I'd have Old Bernice's secret recipe all ready for the haters of Halfway to pick up a fork and take a bite. And I'd make sure Imogene got a big, fat slice.

16

Poop Pie Hits the Fan

My right hand twisted into a useless claw. At least, it felt that way as I scrawled my last *Thanks again! Love, Imogene* on the last pink note card. I stood up to stretch and to shake out the cramps in my fingers.

It was only seven-thirty. The festival should still be going strong, and the first pie-tasting contest wouldn't even start until eight.

I didn't have a dress to wear to the dance, but that was okay 'cause I'm not a dress kind of girl anyway. I threw on my church outfit (a D.A.R.E. T-shirt I'd gotten from school and my American flag shorts) and flew out the door, with my sneaky peach pie in one hand and the paper bag of note cards in the other.

The Halfway Central Park looked downright festive. Paper lanterns hung from tree branches, swaying in the warm autumn breeze. The smells of sugar and spice wafted from a tempting selection of pies arranged on red-checked tablecloths. A large banner hung across the entrance to the park: WELCOME TO HALFWAY'S YIPPIE PIE YAY FESTIVAL. A band made up of mostly old people played an old-timey country song, and pretty much the whole town of Halfway two-stepped under the lights of the gazebo.

A bunch of people smiled at me, and a few even waved. People who weren't even my sorta-friend Francie. Sweat dotted my forehead as I started to have second thoughts about my pie.

"You're late!" Aunt Josephine's voice rang out over the music, and she squeezed my elbow, since my hands were too full for a hug.

"I had to finish some homework."

"Homework on a Saturday night? You've become quite the bookworm."

I wrinkled my nose.

"Pies go there," she said, indicating the long table. "Put it down and then come back to cut a rug!"

Sister Angela-Clarence and Sister Marie Francis caught my eye on the dance floor. Their black wimples stood out against the crowd of colors. (That's what nuns call their head thingies. I Googled it.) They twirled in a country line dance, holding up their long skirts to show off dusty cowgirl boots. I chuckled and nodded.

I'd have to pass the crowded gazebo to get to the long tables, and I had my eyes peeled for Imogene. Maybe I could surrender the finished thank-you cards and she'd leave me alone. Maybe I could catch her rigging the pie-eating contest and blackmail her back. Maybe I could get her to eat a big ol' piece of my peach pie and then ditch the rest so nobody else ate any.

Francie sidled up next to me, chattering in my ear about the band and decorations and the pies. She didn't even say hi anymore, just launched into the conversation right where we'd left off last. Where *she'd* left off last, 'cause I hardly said anything. I couldn't decide if Francie was super-fun or super-annoying. But I didn't want to give her the chance to make any kind of decisions like that about me.

Then a bunch of things happened at once.

Imogene noticed me and made a beeline to get her precious note cards.

I started walking faster, the bag of note cards tucked under one arm, the peach pie in my sweaty hands.

And a big ol' tree root popped out of nowhere and tripped me up good.

The note cards went flying.

The pie went flying.

I went flying.

The music in the gazebo stopped just as Imogene let out a pinched-baby wail. There she stood, right in front of me, the empty pie tin on her head. Peach pie filling and chunks of lumpy crust dripped from her hair. Her hands were clenched at her sides and her eyes were squeezed shut, but she managed to yell through clenched teeth, "You're going to pay for this, Bernice!"

I stumbled to my feet. Francie stood with her hands on either side of her mouth, which was frozen in a perfect O.

"Shoot," I said softly. "I worked hard on that." And then I saw the brown paper bag of soggy envelopes, covered in what was left of the pie. Sigh.

"You did that on purpose!" Imogene choked dramatically on a chunk of crust. I hoped she'd swallow enough to get some of the secret ingredient.

"I surely didn't fall on my face on purpose. I even brought you your dumb cards."

"Well, they're ruined now!"

Everyone stared at us. To them, I was sure it looked like a ginormous bully harassing Halfway Primary's star student. My cheeks got warm, and I stuffed my hands in my pockets and kept my eyes locked on the ground. *Stupid tree root.*

The mayor marched over and made a big fuss about helping his daughter get cleaned up. She cried huge fake sobs. The music started back up in the gazebo, and most folks resumed dancing.

Aunt Josephine appeared and asked me if I was all right.

I nodded, and Francie put her hand on my arm.

"This isn't finished. I'm going to make sure we get to the bottom of this." The mayor's voice was rough and low.

He sounded like someone who was used to getting his way. Just like Imogene.

I thought maybe I'd try a new tactic, something I've never tried before. "I'm sorry. It was an accident. I tripped and the pie flew out of my hands."

"Lies. Nonsense." The mayor put his arm around Imogene protectively.

Aunt Josephine's brows crashed together. "If Bernice says it was an accident, then I believe her." She squeezed my shoulder.

"It's a real act of kindness, you taking in your sister's juvenile delinquent," the mayor said, stepping closer and crossing his arms. "But I have to look out for my daughter. And all the children of this town. You need to make sure you keep this girl under control."

I opened my mouth to say something snarky, but Aunt Josephine beat me to the punch. "Bernice is not a delinquent, and she has been nothing but a delight in our home." Her face turned a funny shade of purple, and her lips pressed into a white line. I looked at her out of the corner of my eyes because I was afraid to look at her straight-on.

She locked eyes with the mayor and said about the worst thing a nun is allowed to say. "Bless your heart."

She said "Bless your heart" just the way Momma does—so it sounds more like a threat than a prayer.

Aunt Josephine had her arm around me tight as a vise. She steered me to the refreshment table and poured me a glass of water. It felt nice to have someone on my side. Almost like when my brothers would help me punch puny kids. But this was different. Aunt Josephine had confronted the mayor to defend me.

I wondered—if she'd known about the secret ingredient in my poop pie, would she have stuck her neck out for me? Darn my devil nature! Why couldn't I show up for a town festival with a tasty laxative-free pie, like what the people of Halfway deserved? Like my aunt deserved? Like Francie deserved?

Imogene seethed at me from across the park, chunks of pie still dripping from her head. I wasn't looking forward to having Imogene as an enemy. She got me madder than a kicked hornets' nest, and Old Bernice wanted nothing more than to squish her like a bug. But for a flickering second I was grateful to her. Because of Imogene and her dumb thank-you cards, nobody had suffered the consequences of my pie. Which meant that New Bernice had Old Bernice in a headlock. For now.

17

Consequences

Almost two whole weeks went by, and the mayor didn't follow through on any of his threats, but that just made me more edgy.

It was like the time Busey got mad at me for flushing all his girlfriend's love notes down the toilet. He'd told me something bad was coming, that I was really gonna get it. I couldn't eat or sleep for weeks. When he finally shaved off my eyebrows in the middle of the night I was almost relieved. At least it was over. At least I didn't have to worry about it anymore.

I kept up with my homework, despite the cloud of doom over my head. Mr. Newton had replaced his hand sanitizer, but he wasn't using it compulsively every time I answered a question.

I got a B on a pop quiz on *The Hobbit*, and Francie showed me her C- before she crumpled it up.

Hot dang, I'd gotten a better grade than Francie.

Huh.

I wasn't used to getting good marks in school. It was weird. This must've been what Oliver felt like all the time.

My riding lessons were going well, and Hoof got a horsey smile on his face whenever I came into the barn. He'd been as gentle as a lamb since that first run across the field. Maybe he wanted to see if I had the right stuff. I guess I passed the test.

Imogene was smug as a bug in a rug, walking around Halfway Primary like she owned the place. She hadn't shown Mr. Newton the picture of me compromising his hand sanitizer, and she hadn't given me any other horrible jobs to do, so I could only assume something worse was coming.

With only an hour left in the school day the last Friday in October, the bored secretary announced the principal wanted to see me. I gulped and headed down the hall.

The secretary had me wait outside the office on a long wooden bench. There weren't any other kids around, so for a lightning-fast second I thought maybe Mr. Jenkins wanted to talk about how well I was doing in school. I could tell from the look on his face when he opened the door that special recognition was *so* not happening.

Mr. Jenkins's office had sickening light green walls, like the color of fuzz that grows on bread. Framed awards and certificates hung all over the place, and a dark wood bookcase sagged against one wall, loaded down with spiral notebooks. It smelled like dirty socks with a hint of new pink eraser.

Three chairs sat on this side of the big wooden desk, and Imogene and the mayor were taking up two of them.

Well, mystery solved. The poo pie drama wasn't over.

Mr. Jenkins gestured to the empty chair before plopping his butt down in his own. He was jumpy and sweaty, and his big square glasses kept sliding off his nose.

Imogene started to cry, dotting at her eyes with a tissue like a granny, and her daddy rubbed her back and gave me the stink eye.

The principal cleared his throat. "Bernice. Imogene. Mr. Mayor . . . I mean, Mr. Franklin. Mr. Rod Franklin . . ." The principal was getting more flustered by the minute.

"Mayor Franklin would be fine." Imogene's dad neatly folded his hands on his lap.

"Yes. Thank you." The principal stared at the pages on his desk. It seemed like every intelligent thought had just flown out of his head.

"We're here to discuss Bernice's attack on my daughter at the pie festival."

"Oh, yes, that's right." Mr. Jenkins smiled, happy to remember what was going on.

"I didn't attack her," I said. "It was an accident."

"So you say," Imogene sniffed.

The mayor leaned in. "There must be something you can do."

"I stayed home from the festival this year, so I didn't see the incident. Also, it wasn't on school grounds and no one was seriously injured."

Imogene broke into another round of fake tears.

"But surely you don't allow your students to go around throwing pies at people." The skin on the mayor's face looked too tight.

"No. No, I guess I don't." Mr. Jenkins shuffled his papers without looking at me.

"It was an *accident*," I said, my voice low and growly. "If I ever attack you, you'll know."

Both of the Franklins' eyes widened. Imogene's hand flew to her mouth.

Mayor Franklin slapped the desk. "A threat. Did you hear that, Jenkins?"

The principal finally looked at me, and I tried to silently plead with him. He didn't know me, but I was really trying here. He shifted on his chair and scratched at his nose.

"This was not an isolated incident. This girl has systematically bullied Imogene since her arrival at this school. She even went so far as to ruin my daughter's birthday."

I bolted out of my chair and clenched my fists at my side. "Everyone loves cheese balls," I snarled. I reached into my jacket pocket and stuffed a handful of stale cheese balls into my mouth, chewing loudly in the mayor's face.

He leaned away from me, covering his nose.

"I am happy to donate to this school on a regular basis,

but only if I am sure that my daughter is receiving the best possible education."

Principal Jenkins cleared his throat. "Sit down, Bernice."

I sank into the hard chair and dug my fingernails into the armrest.

"Due to the circumstances, I'm going to leave *both* girls with a warning. Bullying is not tolerated at Halfway Primary. The next time conflict arises between the two of you, there will be consequences."

Consequences didn't scare me, but dear old Imogene went white as a sheet.

18

Itchy Palms

I kicked rocks all the way home from school that afternoon.

Don't that beat all? For the first time in my life I was trying to be good, do well in school, make friends, and stay outta trouble. And I still found myself sitting in the principal's office apologizing for an honest-to-God accident.

I stumbled as a car whizzed by me on the road. I had half a mind to give up. What was the point, anyway? Momma and Lloyd had most likely spent all my money, and weeks had gone by without adding a single cent to my bank account. If I did somehow manage to scrape together enough cash to get to stunt camp, I was sure Imogene would figure out a way to get me detention over the summer.

I needed some time to myself, so I skirted past the back door of the abbey and pushed through the heavy front doors to the sanctuary.

It was dark and quiet inside. The afternoon light streamed in from the stained-glass windows, and the plank floors creaked beneath my feet. I took a seat in the last row of pews and dropped my backpack at my feet. The sanctuary smelled like old hymnals and lemon wood polish, and it made me tangled-up homesick for the library and Ms. Knightley.

What would Ms. Knightley tell me to do?

She'd say "This too shall pass." And that I shouldn't give up on my dream. She'd say I should use my brains to do what needed to be done. She always called me a resourceful girl.

Well, that was all fine and good for the Old Bernice Buttman. I could solve just about any problem I came across by pounding someone and taking the answer. But the *New* Bernice Buttman was trying hard not to punch anyone. And besides, kindergarten milk money wouldn't be enough to get me to camp.

My thumb smudged a shiny gold plaque on the pew in front of me: DONATED BY THE CONNER FAMILY, 1925. I thought about all those donations for imaginary Farkle, which had never even made it to my stunt camp fund. And that's when I saw the offering basket, sitting up on the table at the front of the church. Sitting all alone up there, like someone forgot to put it away, a beam of sunlight resting on it like a spotlight.

I stood up, but my feet wouldn't move.

There wouldn't be any money inside. Someone was in charge of putting the money in a safe place after the service on Sunday, right? It was definitely empty. I'd take a quick look.

I walked to the front of the sanctuary, and Jesus-on-the-cross gave me the stink eye as I reached for the offering basket. It was full of cash.

My hands started to shake, and I looked around to make sure I was still alone. No one was nearby, but the saints in the stained glass had their eyes on me. Finally some justice for ol' Bernice! A pretty pile of cash left unattended, almost like it was meant for me. Maybe it was payment for all the misdeeds I'd suffered since I'd moved to Halfway. Maybe trying to be a better person really did have its rewards!

Something white poked out of all that green. I pulled out a rumply note in Sister Angela-Clarence's slanted handwriting.

> *"Watch and pray, dear, never get tired of trying, and never think it is impossible to conquer your fault."*
> *—Louisa May Alcott, Little Women*

I didn't want to think about my faults. All I wanted to think about was what would make me happy.

I grabbed up the cash and left the one and only check (*Pay to the Order of Saint Drogo's, Three Dollars and Seventy-One Cents*). The bills felt light in my hand, but when I counted them up, there was nearly two hundred dollars in there.

This was it. The moment of truth. I could shove the money in my pocket and head downstairs. I could deposit my plunder in my bank account and be a whole lot closer to stunt camp. My fingers tightened around the cash and I closed my eyes.

"Aw, nuts."

I threw the sweaty money back in the basket just as the front doors opened.

"Oh, Bernice! I thought you'd be downstairs. What are you doing up here?" Aunt Josephine's face was red and sweaty, and I wondered if she'd just come in from gardening.

"I came in to . . . pray. And then I noticed the offering was left in here. Someone should take care of that."

"Bless you! What an oversight. I'll see that the money gets put away. Heaven knows we need it."

I handed the basket over, and her eyes went to the neatly stacked bills. My palms itched, but I refused to scratch them because that was practically a confession. And I had nothing to confess. "What do you mean, you need it?"

She sighed. "You might as well know. The abbey is in trouble. We barely get enough cash to keep the lights on, and we just got an estimate for roof and heating repairs. If we can't come up with two thousand five hundred dollars by April fifteenth, the town will condemn this building."

Two thousand five hundred dollars. The exact amount I need. I'll be darned.

"What? They can't do that!"

"I'm afraid they can."

"But this is your home."

Aunt Josephine patted my arm and looked up at the Jesus-on-the-cross.

"That's why last week's contributions were so much more than usual." She counted the cash in her palm. "We pleaded with the patrons to dig deep. But we can't every week. God has a plan. He will provide."

I wrinkled my nose. *Sure He will.* Maybe I should put in an order for an even five grand so the nuns wouldn't get kicked out *and* I'd have enough for stunt camp?

"God sees us, Bernice." She had tears in her eyes as she stared at the stained glass.

I thought about what God had almost seen me do a few seconds ago and I shuddered. Stealing from the offering plate. That one would have sent me straight to hell. Whew. Good thing my conscience kicked in at the last minute. Better late than never.

19

Sparks Flying

After a few weeks of me staring at the ceiling, trying to figure out how I could get my hands on five thousand dollars, Imogene decided to get her revenge.

I'd yawned through the chilly November morning in Mr. Newton's class. Halfway through a math quiz, my last pencil tip broke. *Oh, snap.*

I threw a tiny spitball at my desk buddy, Francie, and when she looked up, wiping the slobber off her face, I mimed borrowing something to write with. She searched around her desk (pretty dang loudly, I might add) before shrugging her shoulders and mouthing, "Sorry."

I sat there tapping the nub of my eraser on my desk until Mr. Newton finally looked up. "Are you finished, Miss Buttman?" He still called me Miss Buttman whenever he got the chance.

"Can I sharpen my pencil?"

The sharpener was out in the hallway and shared

between the third- through fifth-grade classrooms. It was a big hassle to get permission to go use it. I don't know what he was afraid we were going to do out there. Although the sharpener *was* temptingly close to the fire alarm.

It was almost like I'd teleported my fire-alarm-pulling thoughts to him, because he shook his head and did his hand sanitizer thing.

"Here, use this." He handed me a pink pencil engraved with PROPERTY OF MR. NEWTON in gold letters. "Make sure you give it back."

I finished the math quiz after a lot of seat shifting and armpit scratching. The fractions threw me for a loop, but I think I did good on the rest of it. Whoever invented fractions could kiss the south end of a northbound skunk.

We handed our papers in, and Mr. Newton twisted his mustache and squinted at me. "Pencil?"

"Oh, right. Sorry." But when I got back to my seat, the pink pencil was gone.

I trudged back up to the teacher's desk as the last of the students filed out the door. "It's gone. I guess I lost it."

He gave me a look so sour I was afraid he was about to grease and flush me. You'd think I'd lost his car or his firstborn kid or something. He turned a sickly shade of magenta while he lectured me on responsibility. My fingers twitched, and I wanted to give him a purple nurple so bad I could taste it. My momma used to say, "If you've got a hammer, everything's a nail." Well, Mr. Newton had the hammer called Bernice Is a Moron, and he was sure pounding me over the head with it.

He asked me to stay in the classroom during lunch, to look for his lost property and think about responsibility. Every time he said the word *irresponsible*, I heard the word *stupid*, and it 'bout made my blood boil. Back home, I ate lunch all by myself darn near every day. But now . . . I would miss Francie. Sometimes she shared her Mountain Dew.

I'd polished off my apple and rolled my paper bag into a ball when Imogene appeared in the doorway of the classroom. Her lips were curled into a snarl, her hands planted on her hips. The only thing she was missing was a mustache to twirl.

"What're you doin' here?" I mumbled.

"Getting the last little bit of pie off my face," she said with a smirk. She walked behind the teacher's desk and threw something small and pink inside his microwave. At first I didn't understand what she was doing.

It was slow motion.

I stood up.

She pressed one minute and the pencil instantly started to flash like a strobe light.

By the time I got over to the smoking microwave, the pink pencil was on fire and our teacher would need a new way to cook his after-school popcorn. Imogene was long gone, of course, and I was standing there, burning my fingers with the evidence, when the fire alarms kicked on.

I covered my ears and tried to make a run for it, but I was halfway out the door when I ran smack-dab into Mr. Newton. He took one look at the smoking pencil in my hand and his smoldering microwave and marched me swiftly to the principal's office.

I couldn't explain to Mr. Jenkins that it was Imogene who had put the pencil in the microwave. First of all, no one would believe me. I was the one who'd last been seen with the pencil. I was the one who'd gotten a huge lecture from Mr. Newton. And Imogene was supposedly a model citizen. So I was toast.

The alarms stopped blaring and the fire department cleared the classroom as "not on fire." I told the firefighter who questioned me I had no idea how the pencil had gotten in the microwave and I'd turned it on accidentally while trying to get it out. He nodded grimly and wrote something in his report.

When Mr. Jenkins got done talking to the firefighters, he joined me in his office. The smell of burnt popcorn followed him through the door.

"I've got your records here, Bernice." Long pause. Long, long pause. Was he gonna kick me out of school? What in the blazes had all those teachers written in there?

"It seems your grades have improved considerably."

I waited for the bad news.

"And you've stayed out of trouble, for the most part. I didn't feel good about that last meeting we had." He let out a long sigh. "Some parents get overly involved in their children's education."

I kept my mouth clamped shut. He was almost being friendly, and I knew if I made a wrong move, I'd be in detention for sure.

"If you say it was an accident, then let's leave it at that. The PTA will buy Mr. Newton a new microwave. The sprinklers didn't go off, and we only missed a small amount of instructional time. I'm glad no one was hurt."

I smiled. *Dang. I'm off the hook.*

But Imogene had just got herself on it like the wiggly worm that she was.

I was having a sort of battle with myself. It was like the time Sue Ellen Eaton and Randy May Clump decided to fill the kiddie pool with Jell-O. It turned into two fat girls tussling in goo, and everyone from the Lone Star Trailer Park gathered round to watch the carnage.

In the first corner was the New Bernice. I wanted to be good. I wanted to stay out of trouble. I wanted Ms. Knightley and Aunt Josephine and the rest of the nuns to be proud of me. I maybe wouldn't even mind if Momma came around sometime and noticed how not-Buttman-like I had turned out.

In the other corner, Old Bernice reared her ugly head.

Imogene was the devil, and when you come face to face with the devil, you'd better give him the what for.

• • • •

I stayed holed up in my room that night, afraid that the nuns might somehow smell the melted plastic aroma that clung to my clothes and want to know what happened. I was so used to lying to get outta trouble, I almost kept forgetting that I really hadn't done anything this time! I left the door to my hidey-hole open, just so I wouldn't suffocate, and so I could keep an eye on Sister Marie Francis, who was acting more jazzed up than a toddler on Pixy Stix.

The old nun would walk by my room and pause at the door like she was dying to ask me something, and then spin on her heels and walk in the other direction. I'd watched her do this at least six times. Either she was trying to wear a rut in the floor, or she had something she wanted to say to me, and I was not about to help her out.

She'd probably gotten a call from Principal Jenkins. She'd probably heard about me almost burning the school down (wait, that was Imogene!). She probably wanted to lecture me on safety, or respect, or . . . Well, I didn't know what, but I wasn't going to say anything to get that ball rolling. I just sat reading at my desk, trying to keep my eyes from drifting to her back each time she spun away from my doorframe.

Finally, she made a noise. It was a kind of loogie sound from the back of her throat, but when I looked up to see if she would say anything, she wasn't exactly looking at me. She was looking at my computer. Looking at it like it was the last slice of pie in an all-night diner and she was waving a fork.

But then she spun on her heels again, and I cocked my head sideways and crunched my eyebrows together until she came back. Which she did, about ten seconds later. I couldn't take the weirdness anymore. "Sister Marie Francis, what in the blazes are you after?"

She wrung her hands in front of her wooden cross necklace and risked a glance at me. "I've been wondering. I mean, I've never tried . . . It's just . . . I don't know how . . ." She trailed off, and a look of panic took over her face. She was drowning in her own words and she was looking to me to throw her a floaty doughnut.

"What is it that you don't know how to do?" I asked, real slow, like I was talking to a skittery animal.

Sister Marie Francis fiddled with the sleeve of her black robe. "Well, it isn't specifically forbidden or anything. Just frowned upon, I guess . . ."

She looked like she might spin away again, so I decided to intervene. "Listen, if it ain't forbidden, it's fair game.

One time my brother Busey brought a possum to school, and when the principal tried to get all high and mighty and tell him he had to kick it out, my brother asked them to point to where it said you couldn't bring a possum to school in the handbook. And the principal and the secretary and Busey's poor frazzled-nerve teacher skimmed through every line of that handbook looking for where it said no possums."

Sister Marie Francis was interested enough to look less seasick. "And did they find it?"

"Course not! They didn't used to have anything about possums in the handbooks! Not before Busey. You better believe it's in there now, though. That possum probably learned more in tenth grade than my brother."

Sister Marie Francis laughed and sat down on the edge of my bed.

"I think I'd like to learn how to use your computer, Bernice. If you could teach me? I want to know how to send email."

I wanted to laugh out loud, 'cause it was such a small thing, but I thought that might scare the nun off. "Of course, I'll teach ya. Email's easy."

Sister Marie Francis smiled and I stood up so she could take the desk chair. I hovered behind her and tried not to breathe stinky breath on her neck like all teachers in the world tend to do.

"Okeydoke. First you gotta turn the computer on. Just jab that button right there."

Sister Marie Francis used a shaking finger to touch the button, but she was so gentle it didn't even pop on!

"You gotta poke it like you mean it. Come on, it's okay. You won't hurt it."

"I just . . . I don't want to break it. Computers are quite expensive, aren't they?"

"Well, I wouldn't drop one off an overpass or anything, but generally speaking you don't have to be as gentle as all that."

She nodded and gave the button a good punch and the screen flickered to life.

"Great!" I said. "Step two is you have to connect to the internet. Click on this circle, right here."

She tried to push the icon like a button. I wanted to laugh so bad, but I remembered all the times I'd fallen off Hoof and how Sister Marie Francis had never even once laughed at me, so I held it in. "You have to use the mouse," I said instead, showing her how. It took her a few tries to get her hand and eye to play nice, but finally she clicked on the icon and we were on the internet.

"Now, do you have an email account?" I asked.

"Yes. It's Jesusismyhomeboy@email.com."

I snickered at that. "Well, then we just go to email.com and enter your username and password and you are all set."

I thought for a second. "You don't have a secret boyfriend you're writing to, do you?"

Marie Francis burst out laughing. "Heavens no! I have a niece in Arizona. She's been bugging me to switch to email, and she set up the account for me. This way, we can keep up with each other better."

I smiled. "That's real nice. She's lucky to have an aunt like you."

Aunt Josephine poked her head in the room. "And you are lucky to have an aunt like me. I just got off the phone with your principal and it seems the fire department was called today."

"It wasn't me! Plus, Principal Jenkins just gave me a warning!"

Both of the nuns shook their heads, but they were smiling.

"I guess there wasn't anything in the handbook about setting fires?" Sister Marie Francis asked.

"I bet there will be next year!" I grinned.

• • • •

Helping Sister Marie Francis with the computer made me feel sparkly and shiny inside. Every couple of days she would come tapping at my door and quietly ask to use my computer. She got so happy when she had an email from her niece, and I felt like I had something to do with that happiness.

The only bee in my bonnet was Imogene. I thought about how I was gonna get back at her for the whole microwave-pencil explosion, but nothing good enough was coming to mind. It had to be something smart but evil, which was not usually my best combination.

It was the Monday after Thanksgiving break, and the leaves crunched under my feet when the idea hit me. I rubbed my hands together and cackled, picturing the Old Bernice with her foot on New Bernice's neck in the kiddie pool, arms raised in victory. Old Bernice smiled and nodded in approval.

The next morning, I sat at my computer and typed a professionally worded letter of congratulations, sealed it in a long white envelope, and stuffed it in my backpack. I ate my oatmeal with a smile.

I got to class early and placed the letter on Imogene's desk before anyone else arrived. Then I went back out and waited in the hallway for the bell to ring.

As the students filed into the classroom, Imogene noticed the envelope right away. She looked around and asked a few kids where it had come from. Everyone shrugged and brushed past her, hanging up their backpacks and taking off their jackets. She stared at her name on the envelope, blinking rapidly.

"Aren't you gonna open it?" one of the girls said.

Mr. Newton scribbled in his lesson plan book and yelled for everyone to read silently for the next fifteen minutes. *Hmm.* Somebody had forgotten to do his lesson plans. *Slacker.*

Imogene ripped open the envelope and smoothed the letter flat on her desk. I watched her out of the corner of my eye as a smile began to spread across her face. I had to work hard to keep my own expression as blank as Momma's acting résumé. Her hand shot into the air.

"What is it?" Mr. Newton sounded annoyed. It was clearly hard for him to get his teacher work done with all these annoying students around.

"I have an announcement."

"It can wait."

"But it's really exciting. I'm sure everyone will want to hear."

He sighed and shook his head. "Fine."

She stood up and walked to the front of the room, the letter fluttering in her shaking hands. She had rays of sunbeams shining out her nostrils, I tell you what.

"Everyone, I just received confirmation that I've been chosen for the Principal's Citizenship Award." She made a squeaky "EEEEE" like somebody beating a granny with a cat.

The class gave Imogene a smattering of applause, and she smiled and bowed and smiled and bowed. Mr. Newton scribbled notes in his planner, and he nodded without looking up.

"This letter from Principal Jenkins says"—she paused dramatically—"and I quote, *Imogene Franklin is the most model student at Halfway Primary.*"

Everyone stared at Imogene, and she thought that meant they wanted her to keep blathering on.

"*She expresses her love of the community by constantly sucking up to teachers and having her father write out big checks to charity.*" Her smile sagged a bit.

The kids whispered to each other.

"What in the world?"

"Sounds about right."

"It also says that as the recipient of this prestigious award, I'll be honored with my own office, right next to the principal's."

I snickered behind my hand, and other people did, too. This was too easy. I never dreamed she'd get up and read the thing in front of everyone!

Imogene looked confused for a second. "The only other office space is the nurse's. . . . Maybe they'll kick her out."

"An office for what?" someone said. "To hang up all your suck-up awards?"

Our teacher finally looked up. "What's this about?"

Imogene showed him the letter. She was practically bouncing out of her loafers. "May I go call my father? He'll be so proud of me."

"They weren't going to announce the winner until April," Mr. Newton muttered. "*The recipient of this special award will get to run extra laps in PE for the rest of the school year.* That doesn't seem right. . . ."

Everyone clapped.

Imogene's eyebrows arched, and she crossed her arms and shifted her weight from foot to foot. "Mr. Newton?"

"Take this letter to the principal immediately."

"So I can call my dad?" she asked.

"So Mr. Jenkins can verify its validity."

Imogene frowned. The class giggled, and one of the boys threw a paper airplane that hit her in the face. Someone called out, "Thanks for rubbing our noses in it, though. Super-fun."

You could see the wheels turning in Imogene's brain as she walked to the classroom door. She paused with her hand on the knob and turned slowly, glaring at me. Angry tears formed in her eyes, and she spun on her heels and stomped out.

I should've been happy about the complete and total victory. I mean, Imogene had thought so much of herself she believed they would kick the school nurse out on the street to give her an office. And she had announced it to the whole class and everyone had laughed at her. *Added bonus.*

But something about the look on her face before she stormed out the door set me on edge. She was mad enough to eat barbed wire and poop nails. And I had the sickening feeling the nail gun would be pointed directly at me.

• • • •

I had a whole hour of Imogene-free school time before they called for me over the intercom. I was to come to the principal's office immediately. My third time in just as many weeks. Sigh. Old Bernice was still getting me in trouble.

I trudged down the hallway, dragging out my last few minutes of freedom. By now Imogene had blabbed everything and I was sure to get busted, not only for the fake letter, but for the flaming microwave, the gluey hand sanitizer, and the cheese ball cake. I was a dead girl walking.

As I wandered into the kindergarten hall, I touched each of the sloppy paintings tacked to the wall. I had a strong longing for the Play-Doh-sculpting, snack-eating, big-brothers-always-looking-out-for-me good old days.

On my very first day of kindergarten, a girl in my class had called me a dumb bunny, and Busey and Chucknorris had thrown her brown-bag lunch in a puddle. At the time I had been so proud to have such big strong brothers sticking up for me, but now, looking at these tiny kids . . . it just seemed mean. And it didn't matter if you were squashing people or writing them fake awards, eventually you got caught and you had to pay the price for all that bullying.

I wondered if anyone would notice if I plopped in one

of those tiny kindergarten chairs and colored for the rest of the day.

My feet slowed, and my hand was hovering on the doorknob when a voice too close to my ear said, "What're you doing here?"

Francie. Dang, I needed to put a bell on that girl to keep her from sneaking up on me.

I snapped my hand off the knob. "Got called to the office."

Francie looked at me sideways. "The office is *that* way." She jerked her head in the opposite direction.

"I know where it is. What're *you* doing here, anyway?"

"I asked to go to the bathroom. Thought you might need a friend."

A friend. My heart did a funny double bump.

"I think what I actually need is a lawyer."

Francie laughed. And a crooked half smile broke out across my face, too. "Maybe you should walk me to the office. Since I'm a new student and all."

"Oh, I could be like an *ambassador*!" Francie flipped her hair in a perfect imitation of Imogene, and we broke into giggles.

Francie walked me all the way to the principal's office, swinging her bathroom pass around her arm like a Hula-Hoop. Having her there made everything seem less serious. So what if I got in trouble? Not like it would be the first time. There was nothing Principal Jenkins could throw at me that I couldn't chew up and spit out.

• • • •

I would have been less stunned if Principal Jenkins had actually thrown something at me. Like a tomato. Or a rotten fish. His news hit me in the face like a water balloon.

"Community service? Can you even do that?" My voice came out all squeaky. "Aren't you 'sposed to keep your punishments confined to school grounds?"

"I've talked to your . . . guardians. They agree this is an appropriate consequence."

Imogene interrupted. "Wait. You talked to our guardians?"

"Imogene, from what you've told me, you and Bernice have battled each other since the first week she arrived, so even though the last known infraction was at her hand, you're both to blame. And you'll both receive consequences."

She started breathing loud and fast, and Mr. Jenkins stood up and told her to put her head between her knees.

"But . . . the pie! And the fake letter! And she ruined my birthday party!"

I scowled at her. Only one of those was on purpose.

The principal sat back down and pretended to be

interested in a stack of papers on his desk. "The fact of the matter is, you two have proved you cannot get along. Working together to help others might be exactly what you need to become friends."

Imogene sat up dizzily. Principal Jenkins saw the identical look of horror on both of our faces and backpedaled. "Or if not *friends*, at least . . . nonenemies."

"My father will not allow this. I will not have this on my record." She crossed her arms and glared at him.

I couldn't resist making her squirm. "Well, I for one look forward to the opportunity to serve my community and make a new friend." I smiled my toothiest smile.

Mr. Jenkins smiled weakly back. "Thank you for the enthusiasm. Any ideas about what kind of project would be a good fit?"

I shrugged. What did it matter? I was just as good at picking trash off the side of the road as I was at scrubbing bathrooms. It wasn't like I could use any of my "more specialized" skills (like giving people swirlies or throwing eggs at cars).

Imogene, of course, had an opinion. "I'm not wearing a hairnet."

Mr. Jenkins nodded. It was nice of him to ask. He could've assigned us whatever he wanted. After all, he was the warden and we were the prisoners. Prisoners don't get to pick their own work detail.

To be honest, community service didn't sound all that

bad. It would get me out of the abbey and away from my piles of homework. And I liked the idea of being helpful. Old Bernice was never helpful, but I had a feeling New Bernice would be Pretty Darn. I remembered teaching Sister Marie Francis how to use the computer. It had felt good to be able to show her, and she squealed and hugged me tight every time her niece replied.

"Mr. Jenkins?"

"What?"

"I got an idea. We can go to the retirement home and help the old folks learn computer skills." I leaned in. "Old folks don't even know how to turn a computer on. And they're always afraid they're gonna break 'em. If they knew how to do email and stuff, they could keep up with their families and maybe they wouldn't be so lonely."

He nodded and wrote something down.

I couldn't read Imogene's face. She was either relieved she wasn't going to be wearing a hairnet, or she was terrified of old people.

"Problem solved." I shrugged.

Imogene's look turned hard. Pretty sure she'd rather walk through a campfire in gasoline underwear than do community service with me.

20

Halfway Paradise

When I showed up to the Halfway Paradise Retirement Village the next Wednesday, I was more nervous than a long-tailed cat in a room full of rocking chairs. Aunt Josephine dropped me off in the church van, and since I was a whole seven minutes early I decided to plop on a bench outside the front of the wide one-story building. I wasn't stalling or nothing, I just didn't wanna give away those seven minutes.

Something crinkled in my jacket pocket and I reached in and pulled out a Hubba Bubba wrapper. I was about to toss it, but then I noticed writing on the back. *Courage, Dear Heart* was all it said. Dang Sister Angela-Clarence! How did she always manage to do that? But somehow the words made me feel a little braver, even though they were written on trash.

Cold air whipped my scarf around my neck, and the smell of snow hung in the air. A few scraggly wreaths were stuck to the brick building, but they looked like an afterthought.

No one in my family had ever lived in one of these places. Buttmans tend to die suddenly, and at a young age. But my second-grade class had made valentines for the residents of a local retirement home one time, and delivering those cards had been kinda fun. Old people smell weird. And they're always pinching your cheeks and calling you the wrong name. But they are usually pretty happy to see you, whoever you are.

A black sedan delivered Imogene to Paradise with one minute to spare. Her hair frizzed free from her braids and her eyes were bloodshot and blinking.

She saw me right away, but she didn't slow down or say hi. She plowed toward the doors, and I had to jump up and hustle to catch her.

Inside Halfway Paradise Retirement Village, a glass cage of tropical birds took up an entire wall. A white-haired lady in a wheelchair sat watching the colorful birds flit around and peck at cones of seeds. The scent of birdcage and Lysol mixed with granny perfume. It sure didn't smell like paradise. Not even a halfway one.

Imogene made a beeline for the reception desk, and I followed her with heavy steps.

"I'm here to volunteer." Her hands shook as she signed her name on the clipboard. The nice receptionist offered her a peppermint, but she shook her head.

I never turn down free candy. I reached over Imogene's shoulder and grabbed a whole handful out of the bowl and stuffed them in my pocket. "Sign me up to volunteer, too. I'm Bernice Buttman. But we're 'sposed to be teaching computer skills. No emptying bedpans or feeding people soup."

The lady's smile sagged on one side for a second, but then she perked right back up. "You're the students from Halfway Primary? Mr. Jenkins called to tell us you'd be coming."

He must not have told her about the mess of trouble we'd managed to create that had resulted in our generous community service. I glanced at Imogene, but her skin was sort of gray and she still wouldn't look at me. She was even more nervous around the old farts than I was!

The receptionist called someone on the phone and held up one finger to tell us to hush. Then she asked us to follow her, and we weaved through a maze of hallways. Residents shuffled along wearing sweaters and slippers. A few were parked in wheelchairs on the way to nowhere. Maybe someone had pushed them to lunch but stopped halfway there and forgot about them? They smiled at us with their denture-y teeth and watery eyes.

The reception lady stopped outside a door and pushed it open for us.

Imogene froze on the spot, so I squeezed past her into the small computer lab. A handful of residents were sitting in front of computers in neat rows. Nobody was typing or looking at the screens, though. They were chatting with their neighbors, hands folded in laps like crinkly haystacks. The chatter died down when they noticed us.

It was real quiet for a minute. I kept waiting for Imogene to talk, and she kept waiting for me to talk. I'd never been in charge of a whole group of people before. Nobody had ever wanted to listen to what I had to say. But I thought about Sister Mary Francis's face, how it lit up like the Fourth of July when she saw that email from her niece. Sure, this whole thing was supposed to be a punishment for me and Imogene, but maybe I could make a few senior citizens smile today. *Courage, Dear Heart.*

I cleared my throat. "Uh, hey, old fogies. Thanks for showing up today. Not that you had anywhere else to go, right?"

A few of the old guys smiled, but one of the ladies fumbled with her hearing aid. "What did she say?" she asked loudly.

Imogene stepped on my heels, shivering and hiding behind me. We couldn't both be chickens, so I guessed I was gonna run the show.

I spoke in a booming voice. "I'm Bernice. Behind me here is Imogene. We're both excellent at computers, so we'd be happy to assist you with whatever you want." A few of the hearing aids screeched, and their owners made more adjustments.

"Raise your hand if you need help."

All the hands went in the air, slowly but surely.

I whispered in Imogene's ear, "Just go up to that grandma and ask what she needs help with. You don't have to do small talk or anything. She won't bite . . . unless you get too close to her dentures." I smiled at Imogene's discomfort. She shuffled over to a white-haired granny and pulled up a chair beside the computer. I picked an almost-purple-haired lady on the other end of the room. No sense in us being too close together if we could help it.

"What can I do for ya?"

"Hello, dear. I'm Ethel, by the way. Pleased to meet you." She smiled at me and I smiled back. "My grandson sent me an email telling me all about this competition he was in last weekend. He kept talking about pictures, but I never saw any pictures."

"Okeydoke." I pulled up her email account. It took her three tries to get her password entered correctly, but once we were in, it was easy to find the email from her grandson. She only had three messages in her inbox.

"It looks like he sent a link to a website. See how it's underlined there? You click on it, and it will take you to the pictures." I clicked on the link, and rowdy rock and roll music blared from the computer speakers. The title of the page read "Baymount High Talent Show and Movie Night," and pictures scrolled by of kids doing all kinds of talents, like singing, karate, and juggling.

"There's Johnny," Ethel said, squinting at a boy in a

white karate outfit. "My, doesn't he look grown up. How old is he now? Ten or eleven?"

Johnny looked at least fifteen, and if he was in high school, he had to be older than eleven, but I didn't correct Ethel. I read the page with growing interest. Apparently, Talent Show and Movie Night was a fundraiser that Johnny's school had put on. The students did a talent show, and then they played an old movie on an outdoor movie screen. They charged admission. The website said they'd raised over five thousand dollars.

Well, butter my butt and call me a biscuit. I finally had a plan.

21

Stunt Riding Is Not for Wimps

My idea was to put a stuntwoman spin on the whole Movie Night idea. The kids of Halfway could demonstrate any action movie skills they might have, and then we'd show a butt-kicking flick on the side of the barn. Action Movie Night was exactly what the abbey needed. Sure, it wasn't a very church-y kind of fundraiser, but I knew the stink of a great idea when I smelled it. This town loved an everyone-participates event (like the Yippie Pie Yay Festival).

All of Halfway would come. Everyone would plop down their five-dollar admission. And we'd have enough money for the abbey's repairs and maybe even enough to provide a camp scholarship for some worthy patron.

I just needed to get the nuns on board.

I decided to start with Sister Marie Francis, because if I was going to do this thing, I'd definitely need her help. How else was I gonna learn a stunt riding routine for my demonstration?

I trudged through the first snow of the season and found her in the barn, brushing down Hoof Hearted. She smiled when she saw me, and the way the sunlight twinkled through the cracks in the wall made her look like an angel.

"Hey there, cowgirl. Wanna go for a ride?" she asked.

"Actually, I was wanting to ask you something."

She raised her eyebrows and waited, her breath coming out in white puffs.

All of a sudden, I was afraid to ask about the fundraiser. It was too big of an idea. What if she said no? What if she told me it was stupid? I swallowed hard and asked the first question that came to mind.

"How'd you learn so much about horses?"

A soft smile filled up Marie Francis's face, pushing aside the wrinkles around her mouth. "Oh, that." She went back to her brushing.

"What? Is it a secret or something? Are you not supposed to talk about your life before you came to St. Drogo's?"

The sister paused in her brushing and looked at a spot on the barn wall above my head. "No, it's just I don't think on it much. It seems like maybe it was someone else's life."

"Let's hear it." A bale of hay sat against the wall and I plopped down on it, watching her work.

"Well, I was raised on a farm, and my daddy worked in a rodeo. He rode bulls. It was dangerous, but also exciting.

I remember swelling with pride every time I watched him ride."

She paused in her talking and in her brushing.

"What happened?" I asked.

"He got hurt." She turned her back on me, and I wondered if maybe she was crying, but when she spun around, Hoof's saddle was in her arms. She heaved it on his back and went about tightening the girth.

"He was never the same after that. I spent a lot of time on my horse, Bandit. Sometimes I'd leave in the morning on Bandit's back and not get home until dark."

"Sounds fun."

"It *was* fun." She smiled, but the smile didn't quite touch her eyes.

"Who taught you all the tricks you know?"

"What tricks?"

I started ticking them off on my fingers. "Jumping over stuff, standing up on the saddle, and jumping on and off the horse while it's galloping."

Sister Marie-Francis's face turned pink. "I don't know what you're talking about."

"Come on. I've seen you jump over stuff on old Hoof here, and I'm sure you know how to do some of those other things. You and Bandit would've gotten bored of regular old riding."

"That was a long time ago." She raised her eyebrows.

"But you *do* know how, don't you?"

There was a pause while she weighed the sin-value of lying.

"Fine. Yes. I know how to do all kinds of stunts. But I'm not sure if I should teach you, if that's what you're getting at."

I had recently decided that trick riding would be a very good thing to add to all my other stuntperson skills (hand-to-hand combat and free-falling). I just had to use every ounce of my Buttman charm to get Sister Marie Francis to show me. I would look excellent hanging upside down off a saddle.

"Teach me? Goodness no. I wanted to hear how *you* learned."

"After my daddy was injured, I started competing in the rodeo as a stunt rider. I was pretty good, too."

"I knew it!"

"Yes, yes. You're very smart. Now, are you gonna get up on old Hoof, or am I?"

I got up on my first try (progress!) and Sister Marie Francis led me and Hoof out of the barn.

"What if I told you teaching me a few of your tricks might help save the abbey?"

"Oh, Bernice, standing up on a saddle never solved anyone's problems."

"It might this time."

The idea spilled out of me then. I chattered on and on about Action Movie Night while Hoof plodded in circles around the snow-blanketed pasture. I mentioned all the different Halfway organizations we could ask to participate and possible movies we could show. I even had a plan for concessions. Sister Marie Francis listened but didn't comment, which made me nervous. So I blabbed even more.

When I didn't have another single thing to say about Action Movie Night, it was quiet.

Marie Francis stopped walking and looked at me. "You think it might work?"

"It's the answer to our prayers."

She nodded curtly. "Well then, we'd better start working on your routine. Stunt riding is not for wimps."

I hopped off the saddle and wrapped Sister Marie Francis in a big hug. I whispered "Thank you" in her ear.

"Don't go thanking me yet," she said. "You still have to ask your aunt."

• • • •

Aunt Josephine was easier to convince than I thought. She jumped on the idea, asking all kinds of questions. I pulled up the website for the Baymount High Talent Show and Movie night and the nuns leaned over my shoulder. Even

Sister Angela-Clarence smiled and nodded, her wrinkled old hands clasped together.

I had, of course, left out the part of the pitch where any money beyond what the church needed would go to my camp fund. I figured we could work out all the details later.

22

Ho Ho Ho

More snow came two weeks after Thanksgiving. I sat in the cozy kitchen of the abbey, watching the fat flakes plop down and wondering if Hoof was keeping warm enough in the barn.

My momma had called earlier that day. She and Lloyd had planned to come home for Christmas, but they'd gotten small parts in a commercial for some diet pills so they decided to stay in California. They were the "befores." It was a big deal, I guess.

So Christmas at the Lone Star wasn't going to happen. I drummed my fingers on the slick wooden table and thought back on all the December twenty-fifths of my whole life.

Every year, Momma stacked old boxes from Aldi supermarket and we strung lights on them, like a tree. Then it was time to go to Great-Aunt Bertha's for dinner. She squeezed my cheeks hard and always commented on how big I'd gotten, but she made the world's best Pinchy Pies.

My brothers would go around fancy neighborhoods, "borrowing" a wreath here, a lawn Santa there, until the Palace on Wheels looked downright cheerful.

Since I would be spending this Christmas halfway to nowhere, I might as well squeeze my lemons and make some lemonade . . . by bringing my most favorite Lone Star holiday tradition to the nuns.

It took an entire morning freezing my butt off in the snow, but I managed to construct the Holy Nativity scene out of stuff I'd "borrowed" from the dump. Some of the figures were a little wonky, being made from toilet seats and lampshades and such, but if you squinted and looked at it sideways, you woulda swore you were in the Little Town of Bethlehem.

The sisters had been out feeding the poor all day. Francie went with them, 'cause she was always doing nice stuff like that. She tried to get me to go, but I told her I had a secret project to work on.

It was dusky dark when the nuns busted through the door, shaking slush off their habits and talking about all the souls they'd helped feed. When I jumped out and screamed "Surprise!" Sister Angela-Clarence had to sit down. She clutched her chest and motioned for me to bring her a glass of water. But Aunt Josephine and Sister Marie Francis looked eager and confused and asked me what the surprise was.

I told them to close their eyes, and I led them back out

the door to the side of the church, where I'd done my day's work. They stumbled and giggled and gripped my arm as we trudged through the drifts. I couldn't wait to show off what I'd made.

When we got to the strip of snow littered with junkyard parts, I screamed "Surprise!" again, and the ladies cautiously lowered their hands.

"Well . . . you've been busy." Aunt Josephine scratched her head and then looked to me for an explanation.

"Oh, darn. I forgot the lights."

I jogged over to my creation and jammed the extension cord into the outlet.

You could practically hear the angel choir sing "Hallelujah."

The lights turned the pile of spare tires and washing machine parts into a twinkling Christmas scene straight outta the Good Book.

"Oh, Bernice," Aunt Josephine said, covering her mouth.

"I know it's a lot of junk, but I'm gonna return it to the dump after Christmas, so don't be mad about the mess."

"It's . . . lovely." Aunt Josephine turned to me with her eyes sparkling and wrapped me in a tight hug. "You took the unlovable and made it into the picture of the hope of the world. That's a special talent."

I grinned and bit my lip.

And then I lit the fireworks.

The cherry bombs did a good job of blowing the baby

Jesus to bits, but it was the M-80s that got the whole ramshackle stable to bust apart.

"Hot dang!" I yelled. The nuns covered their ears as another round of fireworks went off.

When the show was over and the pile of junk was back to being a pile of junk, Aunt Josephine gave me a long look.

"Merry Christmas, Bernice," she said, shaking her head.

"Celebrating with a bang! It's a Buttman family tradition." I beamed. Sister Marie Francis clapped while my aunt wrapped me in another hug. That's one thing about living with nuns; there's never a shortage of hugs.

23

A Nun for Real

The next few weeks went by in a blur of planning and training. It was my job to contact all the local organizations or businesses that might want to participate in Action Movie Night.

Halfway only had one dance studio, but they agreed to come up with a "guns blazing" tap routine (whatever that meant).

The martial arts group, which met on Saturday mornings in the back of Halfway's hardware store, also agreed to do a demonstration. They promised lots of boards breaking and bricks crumbling.

I knew Imogene went to the dance class, but I had my fingers crossed that we wouldn't run into each other too much during the event. Francie yammered on about her karate and said her parents already planned on buying two tickets, plus four more for grandparents. At five dollars a pop, that was a nice chunk of change. For the nuns, of course.

Kids came up to me at school, in the hallways, and on the playground, letting me know they'd be performing with their acting class or they'd be doing a demonstration with their archery club. It seemed that word had spread, and St. Drogo's Action Movie Night was gonna be a walloping success.

• • • •

Something felt lighter at church on that snowy January Sunday. It was the same old people, and the same old Bible reading, but there was also something shiny in the air, just out of reach. I think it might've been hope.

Even though no one mentioned the fundraiser during the service, I knew the nuns had told everyone the plan. It was either sell tickets to this thing or stop being Catholic. I think most people were on board.

I couldn't wait to get out of the stuffy sanctuary and work on more of the details. So far we had fifteen demonstrations signed up, which was twelve more than I'd expected. The event would be held on the church property, so we didn't need any kind of special permits or licenses. The Halfway high school band was even going to learn a mash-up of action movie theme songs. Several of the town's restaurants had mentioned they'd set up food booths.

Things were going so well, I should've known Momma would show up.

She banged on the door of the sanctuary while Father Wilson was still giving his talk. Everyone jumped a mile high because we were half asleep. Aunt Josephine bolted over to the door and slipped out. Her and I knew exactly who was on the other side of that door, and she was the only one running to say hello.

Sister Angela-Clarence leaned over and whispered, "*Let the wild rumpus start!*" right in my ear-hole, and it sent shivers all the way down my spine.

Father Wilson stumbled around for a few seconds before picking up where he left off. To be real honest, he could've been telling us to somersault in our underwear and I wouldn't have known the difference.

Momma was in Halfway.

She was right outside.

Now the real question was, *what did she want?*

The father asked us to rise and then blessed us to go do the Lord's work, waving his arm in the air in the shape of a big old X. A very large woman, Gerty Mills, got up to the organ to sing and play. Her voice warbled off the walls and ceiling, hitting a few sour notes here and there but generally coming from an agreeable place.

Momma burst through the doors, with Aunt Josephine hot on her trail.

"Bernice! Honey, let's get out of here. I'm gonna take you out for some fried chicken."

Everyone spun around in their pews to look at me. To

look at Momma. To see the matching set, her and I. The singer paused long enough to determine it was still her turn, then blared on.

"Church was just finishing up, Carlene," Aunt Josephine whispered fiercely.

"Bernice don't care about church," Momma said with a smirk.

I slumped down in my pew, wishing I could melt away. I hadn't seen her in months, but I sure wasn't about to go running to her arms. She didn't care about interrupting Father Wilson's homily (that's the word for a Catholic sermon. I'd Googled it) or ruining Miss Gerty's singing. And I can tell you for sure, she didn't mind embarrassing me.

It would be quicker and easier to give her what she wanted, so I ducked out without looking at anyone. I wouldn't be standing with the sisters at the end of service, saying goodbye to everyone. I wouldn't shake their hands or tell them I'd see them next week. It made me feel droopier than Sue Ellen Fester's skin after her weight loss surgery.

As soon as we were outside and the double doors had slammed behind us, I turned on her.

"What're you doin' here?"

"Now is that any way to greet your momma?" She leaned in and I couldn't take my eyes off a huge hunk of brown stuck between her two front teeth. "Haven't seen you in months, child. Come give me some sugar."

I let her squish me in a stiff hug, but I kept remembering the day she'd found out about Farkle and how she'd squeezed my arm and made me cry. I felt like crying again.

"Isn't anyone feeding you here? You shrunk."

I looked down and sure enough, I could see my own two feet. I guess all those ham sammies and horse riding lessons had whittled my waist. I shrugged. "I eat just fine. Aunt Josephine doesn't buy cheese balls, though. Or soda. Don't miss it as much as I thought I would."

"Look at you, living like a woman of the cloth. Do they got you praying ten times a day and shining up their crucifixes?"

I pulled my ear. Everything's a joke to her. I always feel like she's making fun of me, one way or another.

"It's fine, Momma. I don't mind it. Why are *you* here?"

She straightened up. "I've come to fetch you. California didn't work out for Lloyd and me. We decided to come home to our people."

Home.

The word rattled around in my brain. Where was home? Back to the trailer with my rowdy brothers and my musty couch-bed? Back to a school where I was just a big bully? Back to eating cheese balls out of the tub by my lonesome on a Sunday morning?

"What if I don't want to come with you?" I said it quietly, testing the waters.

Momma's laugh boomed. "What you talking about, you

don't wanna come? You wanna live here forever? You gonna become a nun for real? Oh my God, I gotta call Lloyd. He will not believe they turned you into a real nun."

I let out a long breath in the form of a raspberry. "No, I don't wanna stay forever. But maybe a few more months? I've been working on this project to help the nuns."

Momma's laugh erupted again.

"Helping the nuns. Don't suppose the nuns want help from a ne'er-do-well like you."

My chin jutted out. "I *am* helping them. I'm planning an event to help them raise money so they can pay off their debts. Everything's going great. I just need more time."

She shook her head and let out a low tsking sound. "You always could get people to part ways with their money. When is this event?"

"It's in April."

"All right, Bernice. I'll see you then. Make sure your halo is nice and shiny when I drag your butt back to the Lone Star."

I watched Momma's wide backside retreat down the sidewalk and I wished Action Movie Night was a whole year away.

24

Forget the Fear

Sister Marie Francis insisted I up my riding lessons to every day after school, even though it was crazy cold. She had a boatload to teach me, and only a few short months to do it in. I hoped I could somehow get in touch with my inner cowgirl before then, so I could pull off an amazing routine that would impress everyone.

Hoof Hearted liked all the extra sugar cubes and carrots, but he was not a fan of practicing the same moves over and over again in the snow. He would sometimes stop midtrot and shake his mane or neigh loudly when I'd ask him to pick up the pace.

"That's it, Bernice, just like that! Now swing your left leg up and over Hoof's head. Your *other* left leg!"

My left leg (which turned out to be my right leg) didn't quite clear his ears, so instead of ending up backward on the saddle, I sorta slid off the side. Hoof ducked and stomped his feet as soon as he was freed from my weight. I lay there in the muddy snowdrift, wondering how important it was for the stunt rider to actually stay on the horse.

"Try again," Sister Marie Francis barked. I think she had a past life as a drill sergeant she wasn't telling anyone about.

"I mighta pulled a hammy," I muttered, limping to my feet and rubbing my leg.

"Suck it up, Buttercup."

The old broad was hard as nails. I sighed and stuck one foot in the stirrup and swung myself onto old Hoof's back. "Let's do it again, 'kay, horsie? But with less falling and more spinning."

He grunted, so I guessed he was up for it.

I gave him a nudge and we went from a bouncy trot to an all-out gallop. My butt was barely in the saddle anyway, but swinging my leg over his head without sliding off seemed darn near impossible. I took a deep breath, closed my eyes, and pretended I was spinning around on a stool. A really bouncy stool that might possibly want to kill me.

I managed to kick Hoof in the side of the head, which made him jerk, which made me slide, and I found myself licking slush again.

"Better. You almost cleared him that time."

"Should I be wearing a helmet for this?"

Putting myself in all this danger reminded me of my older brothers. They were always doing risky stuff for no good reason. Like the time the bug zapper on the back deck stopped working and they decided the only way to keep our trailer bug-free was to rig up a flamethrower out of a bike handlebar, a can of hair spray, and a lighter. Busey lost all the hair on his arm, and Gordon singed his eyebrows. But they got the job done. No mosquito dared to cross our trailer's door. I'd get this job done, too, 'cause I'm a Buttman. And we get 'er done.

"Helmet. Hmm. I'll look into that," Aunt Josephine said, and she offered me her hand. I stood up and stretched a minute and gave my brains a good shake before I stuffed my foot into Hoof's stirrup again.

If only I could make money by the bruise.

Hoof took off across the field, and I tried with all my might to swing my leg over without sliding off, and I was halfway successful. Close but not close enough. I found myself spitting out mud while a certain palomino's tail smacked me in the face.

Sister Marie Francis came and sat down next to me on the ground. She squinted up at the cloud-smudged sky and let out a long sigh. "You gotta give it your all. You can't be scared. It's trying to do it slow and careful that's messing you up."

I crossed my arms. "I don't feel like I'm being careful."

"Did you ever get close to dying? Where you thought it might be the end?"

I got a flash of memory. Seeing my breath come out

in a little puff, my fingers blue with cold. My brothers were playing hide-and-seek at the Walmart, and Busey had talked me into crawling inside the freezer, right next to the frozen pizzas. He'd skipped off to find a better spot, and I'd gotten cold, and then sleepy. Thank goodness a lady had reached to the back for a stuffed-crust pepperoni, or I might've been worm food. I tried to focus on the fear in the memory, the frozen fear lodged in my stomach as the snot froze under my nose.

I nodded numbly at Sister Marie Francis.

"You've got to forget the fear. Push through it. Swallow it down and get your body to do what it needs to do. Can you do that?"

I had no idea what she was talking about, but I nodded and blinked at her.

"Forget the fear," she whispered fiercely as she helped me into the saddle and gave Hoof's rump a slap.

Forget the fear. Forget the fear. I looked down at my hands gripping the reins so hard my knuckles were white.

Forget the fear. I relaxed my grip.

I closed my eyes and focused on the beginning of the near-death memory. The part where my brothers played with me and I had an awesome hiding place. I smiled at the thought.

In one quick movement I swung my right leg around, clearing Hoof's head, and then my left leg swung around his rump. I gripped the saddle's edge and tried to find my new rhythm riding backward. *Backward!*

It was fun for about half a minute, and then I forgot to forget the fear and I 'bout peed my pants. *I was riding a horse backward.* Dang, my brothers would've been proud. It made me miss them like a fat kid misses cake.

25

Hobbit Hole

The next day at school, my mind kept drifting back to those few amazing seconds where it was just me and Hoof's rump, bouncing across the pasture backward. I was the leading lady *and* the stunt girl for this particular daydream, and doing a bang-up job. In the dream version of yesterday's events, I didn't even fall on my face. I spun back around in the saddle and gently pulled the reins with a "Whoa boy," and Hoof skidded to a graceful stop. Then I pulled out my rocket launcher and aimed it at the bad guys who'd followed me across the frozen tundra. "Don't mess with 'Merica!" I said before blowing them to smithereens. "BOOM!"

The class burst into nervous laughter, and I felt my cheeks go scalding hot.

Not out loud! Why can't I daydream quietly?

Mr. Newton glared at me. "Something you'd like to share with the class, Miss Buttman?"

"Sorry, sir," I mumbled, slumping down in my chair. Francie gave me a sympathetic smile.

The teacher cleared his throat. "As I was saying." He paused to give me a heavy look. "Now that we've finished *The Hobbit*, it's time to do our concluding project. You can pick any topic related to the book and write two hundred words about it. Then you'll present your essay to the class."

Brandon (a boy who drove the teacher even more bonkers than me) raised his hand.

"Yes, Brandon."

"What do you mean, 'any topic related to the book'?"

"I mean pick anything you read in *The Hobbit* and write two hundred words about it."

Brandon wasn't done. "So if I want to write two hundred words on what a hobbit hole looks like, I can?"

Mr. Newton nodded wearily.

Other kids chimed in. "Can I write about dragons?"

"Can I make up riddles like Sméagol?"

Mr. Newton reached for his hand sanitizer. "Yes, yes. Those are all fine ideas. Just have it on my desk by next Friday."

I frowned and scribbled ideas in my green notebook. The essay would be easy—fun, even. But getting up in front of the class to present it? Let's just say it curdled my guts.

• • • •

So for the next week, if I wasn't working on St. Drogo's Action Movie Night, volunteering at Halfway to Paradise, or falling off Hoof during riding lessons, I was pecking at my keyboard, working on my *Hobbit* paper.

Friday morning was presentation day. I pulled my hair into a side pony and smiled at my reflection. Freckles splashed my cheeks from being out in the sun so much, and my dimples looked cute when I smiled. I didn't look scary anymore. I was losing my edge.

Francie bounced up to me the second I walked in our classroom. "Did you finish your essay?" she breathed.

"Yeah, I did. You?"

"I stayed up until three in the morning writing it under my covers by flashlight. But this morning I tried to read what I'd written. . . ."

She held out a notebook full of blue-inked words written at funny angles in messy, scrawly handwriting. I squinted at the lines, hoping to be able to help figure out what she'd written, but after a few minutes I shrugged and handed it back.

"Lemme see yours," she said as I unloaded the stuff from my backpack. I did *not* want to hand her my typed-up paper after seeing the mess she was fixin' to hand in, so I said I wasn't sure where I'd put it. Her eyes looked unfocused and glassy, but she nodded and plopped into her seat.

The presentations started right after attendance.

James Freeder's paper was about the characteristics of Bilbo Baggins and what made him a great hero. Mr. Newton beamed from his desk. That man must have been part hobbit.

Sandy Hamburg wrote her entire essay about New Zealand, even though that was not technically in the book, it was only where the *Hobbit* movie was shot. Mr. Newton crunched his brow and twirled his mustache.

Francie's name was called, and she swallowed so hard I could hear the spit hit the bottom of her stomach. It took her three tries to stand up, her knees were shaking so bad. I gave her an encouraging nod as she headed to the front of the room.

She talked for five whole minutes about how the Shire represented a more simplistic, less commercial life, and how hobbits were basically the opposite of humans, who were always so worried about buying stuff. By the end of her speech, Mr. Newton was nodding in agreement, but when she handed him her paper, he stopped. "Oh, my," he said quietly. Francie collapsed in the seat next to me and punched me in the arm. "You're next."

My chest tightened like Momma trying to squeeze into last year's leggings. The thudding in my ears was louder than Chuck Norris beating a punching bag. The real Chuck Norris, not my dopey brother. I wiped my sweaty hands on my pants and waited for Mr. Newton to call my name.

I decided right then, I was done being scared of these

kids. They could laugh at me or ignore me all they wanted. I was Bernice Freaking Buttman. I'd done a great job on my assignment, and I was not gonna get my Underoos in a twist reading it to a bunch of half-asleep fifth graders.

My name was called.

I took a deep breath.

I walked to the front.

And I smiled.

"If I had a magical ring, I wouldn't want it to make me invisible. Too many people are already invisible because they aren't popular or rich or smart. I would want the ring to make me kind. That might not sound like much of a superpower to you, but it sometimes feels as impossible as superhuman strength or flying powers or something to me. When you are raised to only think about yourself and getting what you want, you don't turn out to be a very nice person. Nice people think of others and try to make friends. Nice people help out when they can and give people honest compliments. Yes, if I had a magical ring, I would want it to make me kind."

Mr. Newton's eyes were wide behind his glasses, and he snapped his mouth shut as I handed him my essay. "Excellent, Bernice," he said gruffly.

I sat down smiling, because for once he hadn't called me Miss Buttman.

26

Partners in Crime

There'd been an awed silence after I turned in my paper and took my seat. I wondered if it was because they were surprised by what I'd written, or because they'd never heard me say so many words in a row before. The rest of the presentations had been passable, but no one else had gotten Mr. Newton to make that bug-eyed stare. I think he was warming up to me.

I kicked rocks on the way back to St. Drogo's, my mind on magic rings and being nice and making friends. Before Francie, my brothers had been my only friends. Friends that would duct-tape you to a lamppost and leave you there, but at least they would laugh about it. About you. Hmmm, maybe I needed to rethink what a friend does.

Gravel crunched behind me, and Francie and her bouncing red curls sidled up next to me.

"I liked your essay, Bernice," she said. Her face was serious as a heart attack, so I figured she wasn't making fun of me.

I smiled a little. "Thanks."

"I'll tell you a secret, though. I already think you're a nice person."

I snort-laughed.

"I mean it! You don't always *do* nice things or *say* nice things, but I'm sure that on the inside you're *thinking* nice things, right?"

The short answer to that would be *no*. And Francie didn't even know half of the super-mean stuff that Old Bernice had done. But since she was the only person in the running for being my friend, I let it go.

She smiled. "Hey, you wanna do something fun?"

I had a million more emails to send out about St. Drogo's Action Movie Night, but fun sounded like fun.

"What did you have in mind?"

"Do you got a quarter?"

The two of us went to the Halfway Central Park and found a sunny patch of walking trail, and that's where we glued all the change money we'd found in Francie's couch (because, of course, I didn't have a quarter). Then we hid in the bushes and watched people get excited about finding a whole pile of dropped money, only to spend a whole lot of minutes bent over trying to pick it up. We rolled in hysterics, trying not to make a sound.

I wondered if tricking people might fall into the category of Stuff Old Bernice Would Like. But every time I looked over at Francie, smiling and laughing like we were for-real friends, I decided minor pranks were a small price to pay.

When stuck-to-the-ground money got boring, we snuck into the school (which wasn't hard, all the doors were still unlocked for after-school clubs and stuff). Francie kept watch while I set all the clocks forward an hour.

New Bernice didn't feel the slightest bit bad about that one because it didn't even count as breaking and entering. There would just be some head-scratching involved, and that seemed harmless enough.

Then we went back to the abbey and Googled stuff. (What makes horses drool? How far is it to the center of the earth? Who is the richest woman in the world?)

When our fingers were tired of typing and our sides hurt from laughing, we went to the Dairy Queen and had dipped ice cream cones (Francie's treat!). We decided to take them down to the creek, even though it was still cold outside.

The January sky was dark blue and the clouds puffed white. The wind turned our cheeks pink, but the ice cream tasted too good to stop eating, even when our teeth started to chatter. The creek made a happy sound that reminded me of a baby gurgling.

"I've lived in Halfway my entire life, and I don't think

I ever had so much fun as I did today." Francie zipped up her jacket to block the wind.

I smiled. The coins and clocks were kid's stuff compared to the capital-T Trouble me and my brothers could get into. But it was fun hanging out with Francie, no matter what we were doing. It was nice to have a partner in crime.

She ate the last bite of her cone. "Mr. Jenkins is gonna freak out when he walks in tomorrow morning and thinks he's an hour late!"

"He'll figure it out when he looks at his watch. Still pretty funny, though." My cone was gone, too, so I crumpled the wrapper into a ball and stuffed it into my pocket.

She stared out at the water. "So, do you miss your home and your family and stuff?"

Momma. Buttman brothers. Moldy couch.

"I guess. A little."

"But you aren't going back, right? You're gonna stay in Halfway?"

I remembered Momma's joke about me becoming a nun and living here forever. Was that what I wanted? I wasn't sure. Definitely no to the becoming-a-nun part. There were a lot of good things about living in Halfway. Francie might be one of them. And it was all going by so fast. Just like the stream rushing by in a blur of brown near our shoes, my time here in Halfway slipped away faster than I could catch it.

"Probably not. I don't know." No sense in her worrying about it. But Momma had said that after Action Movie Night she'd come take me back to the Lone Star. I wondered if my bank account would at least have enough money to pay the deposit for camp by then.

27

Betting All the Bananas

February blew in cold and wet. My riding lessons earlier that day had included fat raindrops melting down my spine, so I was grateful for the warm glow of St. Drogo's kitchen.

The nuns were gathered around the table, but instead of eating dinner, they were playing cards.

"I'll see your Chiquita and raise you a Rio." Aunt Josephine slid something small across the tabletop without taking her eyes off Sister Marie Francis.

I squinted at the pile of paper ovals. "What are those?"

"Banana stickers," the two speaking nuns barked at the same time, studying each other furiously for a crack in their perfect poker faces.

I snort-laughed. "My brothers play with beer-bottle caps. They're a lot easier to come by in a trailer park than in an abbey, though."

Sister Marie Francis held her cards close to her chest. "Sister Angela-Clarence has a collection of over fifteen different brands. She started saving them when she lived in Mexico."

Shoot. I didn't even know the silent old nun had lived in Mexico. It was hard to get to know someone who only talked in book quotes. It's not like the Grimm brothers had ever started a fairy tale with "Remember those years I lived in Mexico?"

"Quit stalling and show us what you got!" Josephine said, and all the nuns slapped their cards down at the same time.

"Two of a kind!" said Sister Marie Francis.

"Full house!" Aunt Josephine crowed.

We all turned to look at the fan of cards Sister Angela-Clarence had slid across the table.

"What?" I asked. "What happened?"

"Royal flush! How does she keep doing that?" Sister Marie Francis griped.

"Every dang time," my aunt said.

The sisters grudgingly gathered up the deck while Sister Angela-Clarence put the ovals into a neat pile. She beamed at me and waggled her eyebrows.

"Deal me in," I said.

My aunt looked at me skeptically. "Do you have any banana stickers? You gotta have something to ante up with."

I walked over and peeled six Chiquita labels off the browning bananas on the counter.

"Chiquitas are the most common, therefore worth the

least. Think of them like pennies," Sister Marie Francis said. "On second thought, don't think of them like pennies, because then this might be considered gambling. Think of them as trash you'd throw away and don't care about at all."

Aunt Josephine nodded in agreement.

"Okay, so I have six Chiquitas to wager—"

"Not wager, *play with*," Sister Marie Francis interrupted.

I flared my nostrils. "*Play with.*"

My aunt shuffled. "That's wonderful, dear. The loser has extra kitchen duty for a week." I gulped. I only barely knew how to play poker.

"This is five-card stud, deuces are wild. Everybody in," Aunt Josephine said.

We all slid one Chiquita sticker into the pile in the middle. Well, they slid theirs—mine stuck to my fingers and I had to peel it off me and stick it on the table. All the other stickers had been stuck to paper and carefully cut out. These chicks were serious about their nongambling poker chips!

Josephine dealt each of us one card facedown. I peeked at mine. It was a three. Hmm. Not the best start. Everyone pushed one more banana sticker into the pile.

The next round was passed, and then the next. I now had a three, an ace, and a two. Ace, two, three was some kind of straight, right?

Round four gave me another ace, so at least I had a pair. The nuns were only betting one Chiquita apiece, and no one upped the ante, because they wanted me to be able to stay in the game. If anyone raised, I'd have to fold, because I only had a few stickers left.

In the last round I got another two. Two pair and a three. It was too late to cheat, and I wouldn't know exactly how, but I couldn't help scowling at the look of triumph on Aunt Josephine's face as she displayed her hand. "I've got a straight."

Sister Angela-Clarence had not fared as well this round. She'd only gotten two of a kind.

I plopped my two pairs down, prepared to be stripped of my hard-earned banana stickers.

"You've got four of a kind!" Aunt Josephine's mouth sagged open.

"Just two pairs."

"Deuces are wild, sweetie. Add those to your pair, and you win the whole shebang." Sister Marie Francis looked pleased that at least it wasn't Sister Angela-Clarence adding to her sticker pile. My aunt pouted. "Beginner's luck."

"Two out of three?" I said, and Sister Marie Francis grinned as she scooped the deck together and started shuffling. "It will be much harder to keep that poker face when you actually know the rules."

We played a few more rounds, each of us taking the pot

at least once. Aunt Josephine scrunched her eyebrows at her hand and spoke without looking up from her cards. "If we don't raise the money . . . if the abbey has to close . . . what will you do, Marie Francis?"

I gulped. I didn't want to think about the abbey closing.

"I'd ask to be reassigned, I guess. Imagine that, a whole new abbey and a whole new batch of old broads to get used to."

My aunt laughed and raised by two Chiquitas. "It would be like trying to be grafted into a whole new family, wouldn't it."

Now, that was something I could understand.

We all looked at Sister Angela-Clarence and tried to picture her living in a new place, with new people. What if they didn't know she liked the skin peeled off her apples? What if they didn't let her keep the temperature up just a little too high? And what if they didn't recognize her book quotes? She would lose her home and her family and her voice. I placed my cards facedown, foldin' cause they mostly stunk, but I would not give up on saving St. Drogo's. I was going to raise that money so the nuns could keep their home.

We all groaned when we realized we'd lost yet another hand to Sister Angela-Clarence. She scooped up her winnings, smiled, and said, "*My mom says some days are like that.*"

"*Winnie-the-Pooh?*" Aunt Josephine asked no one in particular.

I remembered sitting on Momma's squishy lap, helping her turn pages in a beat-up picture book. "I think it's from *Alexander and the Terrible, Horrible, No Good, Very Bad Day*. Used to be one of my favorites."

Sister Angela-Clarence smiled and tapped her nose, like I'd gotten it right on the nose. I decided to forgive her for kicking our heinies at poker and taking all of our loot. Especially because her future home and happiness all rode on the success of my wacky fundraiser.

It was like Aunt Josephine could read my mind. "People all over town are excited about St. Drogo's Action Movie Night. It was a stroke of genius, Bernice." She dealt what she promised would be the very last hand of Texas Hold 'Em.

I smiled. "Statistically, I was bound to have a good idea at one point in my life."

She didn't take her eyes off her cards. "Well, I'm glad I was here to witness it."

I grinned and bet all my banana stickers on my hopefully winning hand.

28

Bernice Buttman, Model Citizen

By the end of February the snow was finally gone and I was able to up my riding lessons to two a day, so I'd be ready for my first big performance. I didn't mind the extra time with Hoof and Sister Marie Francis, but my backside wasn't enjoying its extra rendezvous with the ground. After planting myself in the mud a few thousand times, I was dismissed. So Hoof and I headed to town, to escape the peace and quiet of the country.

We trotted past the school and the neat homes of Halfway until we came to the town square. I remembered the guy on the horse in the ice cream shop's drive-through, but I decided my camp fund needed every cent it had. Until after Action Movie Night, anyway.

The town square was busy, even for a Saturday afternoon, and when I rounded the corner I saw a herd of small kids running around the courthouse lawn. Only one voice attempted to calm the chaos.

"Everyone, sit down. Sit down now!" Imogene sprinted from shrimpy kid to shrimpy kid, touching their shoulders and yelling at them to sit. The adults looked mildly amused.

Hoof and me decided to investigate. We trotted up to the courthouse lawn and a truck honked at us as we left the crosswalk. The kids turned to see what the honk was about, and suddenly snot-nosed brats surrounded Hoof and me.

"I like your horsey."

"What's his name?"

"How'd you learn to ride him?"

I hopped down and lightly held Hoof's bridle so they could pet his velvety nose.

"Stay away from his hindquarters," I told them knowingly.

"Will he kick us?" A little boy pushed his glasses up his nose, his eyes wide.

"Naw." I leaned in like it was a secret. "But he toots when he's nervous."

The kids erupted in giggles and pinched their freckly noses between twiggy fingers. I smiled and realized I didn't want to sit on any of them. They were kinda cute. And I doubted they had much cash, anyway.

"Everyone, come back to the grass. We need to start our program." Imogene glared at me, and she tried to get them to follow her, but they stuck to me and Hoof like ticks on a dog.

"Did you start your own day care or something?" I asked Imogene.

She crossed her arms. "This is a day camp I organize. I watch the children so their parents can shop. The Halfway Chamber of Commerce said it was the best service project they'd ever been proposed."

"Good for you." I smirked.

"It *is* good for me. It shows what a good citizen I am."

"I thought you already got that award."

She glared at me. I glared at her.

"Can you leave now, so I can get them to come back to the grass?"

My eyes narrowed at the scrunched-up set of Imogene's shoulders, and something inside me went mushy. I gave Hoof's flank a pat. "I have a better idea. How 'bout I stay and help you? I could give the kids horse rides."

"No. I don't need any help. Thank you."

Just then one of the little booger-eaters came running up to Imogene with brown streaks all over his nose. "Samson stuck my face in dog poop again!" he wailed.

Old Bernice chuckled at the kid's misfortune, but New Bernice crossed her arms and shook her head. I remembered Oliver's angry face, dangerously close to poo, and for once, I wished I'd done something different.

"Which one is Samson?" I was surprised to hear myself ask.

The little guy, whose name was Douglas, pointed me to a scowling boy in a dirty superhero T-shirt.

"Cool shirt," I said, and the kid was so surprised he wasn't getting in trouble the scowl wiped right off his face. "You like superheroes?" I asked.

Samson nodded, suddenly shy.

"Me too," I said, patting Hoof. "But you know what's even cooler than a guy with superpowers?"

Both kids shook their heads.

"Regular people who fight crimes and help people and they don't have any kind of powers at all. They have to have the strength in here"—I jabbed my chest—"to make the world a better place and stuff."

The boys nodded solemnly and I leaned toward Samson. "Hey, lay off the shrimp, okay? Try being nice. It makes you feel better." I gave Imogene the side-eye and a cheesy smile.

Imogene expertly pulled a wet wipe out of her pocket and handed it to Douglas, but then she sighed. "Fine. You can stay."

I spent the afternoon helping the citizens of Halfway. And I didn't expect anything in return. New Bernice did a touchdown dance inside my chest.

29

Patching Things Up

Weeks later, I couldn't shake the picture of that little boy with dog doo all over his nose. I figured Oliver had long forgotten me by now, but maybe I could still do the right thing.

I sat at my computer and clicked away, picturing my old friend Oliver and hoping my email found him happy and healthy.

Dear Oliver,

This is Bernice Buttman, and I am writing to apologize to you for any and all attempts to bully you. I realize now that it was wrong and probably hurt your feelings (and your person). Please forgive me for the following infractions:

Telling the whole class you had head lice.
Swapping out your sunscreen for porch paint.

Tying your backpack to the back of the school bus.
Putting crickets in your desk.
Putting slugs in your pockets.
Making you kiss that dead squirrel.
Telling your mom I was your girlfriend.
Telling everyone I was your girlfriend.
Sitting on you on the playground.
And threatening to stick your nose in poo.

Your friend,
Bernice Buttman

Oliver replied a few days later.

Dear Bernice,

You are the worst girl I ever met. I do NOT forgive you for any of that stuff. I donated my whole summer's worth of lawn mowing money to help your dumb dog and then you left and I never even got to see what he looked like with his brand-new smile. You need Jesus, Buttman.

I sighed and logged out of my email. Me and Jesus were fine, but it seemed me and Oliver might never patch things up.

30

To the Rescue

On the first Saturday in April the property surrounding St. Drogo's Catholic Church hummed with activity. People had been setting up for Action Movie Night for days, and things were finally starting to come together. A big long stage was built in front of the double doors of the barn, and a movie screen hung above. The movie theater donated life-sized cutouts of Rambo and Tom Cruise from *Mission: Impossible* and a popcorn machine, which waited off to the side.

The Halfway High School had allowed us to borrow two sets of bleachers, which stood just outside the pasture. In a few short hours, those seats would be full of paying customers and Action Movie Night would be off and running.

The nuns and I bustled around the barn, telling people where they could set up their stuff and change into their costumes. Hoof whinnied nervously from his stall, and

I petted him on his soft nose. "It's okay, boy. Just some extra people hanging around. No need to be scared." But I could feel the nerves bundling up in my belly like twisted tree roots. Tonight I would show the town of Halfway my stunt riding skills. And by the time we wrapped this thing up, I'd have a pretty good idea if camp was happening for me or not. It was an important night.

Sister Angela-Clarence slipped a note into my hands before she disappeared in the crowd. It read:

> *Then it was that there came into my head the first of the mad notions that contributed so much to saving our lives.*
>
> *—Robert Louis Stevenson, Treasure Island*

She thought my mad notion might save our lives. No pressure or anything.

Francie bounced into the barn, already wearing her white karate outfit. She gave a mighty yell and chopped at my arm, but I licked my finger and stuck it in her ear, which got her to back away quick. "Eww, Bernice! That's not the way of the samurai!"

"Well, it worked, didn't it?" I grinned at her, and she stuck her tongue out at me. The rusty old clock announced we only had a few minutes until the program kicked off. Literally. The kids from the Halfway Karate School were the first performers on the program.

"Are you nervous?" I asked Francie. She nodded at a few other kids wearing the same white robe that she was.

"Naw," she said. "I'm only breaking boards. I've been able to do that since I was five. How about you?"

"I've broken lots of stuff since I was five."

Francie laughed. "No, silly. Are you nervous about your routine?"

I glanced over at Hoof Hearted, who stood in his stall with his ears plastered back. "Maybe a little. Don't tell anyone. I've had some trouble with my last trick—standing up on the saddle."

Francie looked impressed. "Woo-eee, that's sweet. I mean, as long as you don't fall on your butt it will be."

I scowled. I'd been working on the stunt for months and I still never managed to stand all the way up. Most of the time I fell off in the attempt. Sister Marie Francis thought I should drop it from the routine, since I'd never done it successfully.

I was gonna tell Francie that the whole standing thing might not happen, when I heard a familiar voice screech from the stage. I hurried out the wide double doors to find Imogene looking madder than a kicked-over hornets' nest, wearing a sparkly black-and-white dance costume and yelling at a blond girl.

"You had one job, Greta. One job. I can't believe you're ruining this for me."

"I'm sorry! I was sure the CD was in here." The blond

girl lifted the lid of the player as if the music might be hiding inside.

"Now the whole routine is ruined! Our entire troupe will be humiliated."

"I could run to the dance studio and see if the CD was left in there?" The blond girl looked seriously scared of Imogene, which was probably smart.

"There isn't time! They're going to start seating people in a few minutes. What if the CD isn't in the studio?" Imogene got real tears in her eyes. "My dad's coming to watch me dance. You've ruined everything."

I thought about Mayor Franklin's stern, thin mouth and hard eyes, and for some reason I wanted to help Imogene. I mean, she was one of my least-favorite people ever, but I could feel New Bernice springing into action.

"What's the song called?" I asked. She blinked her watery eyes at me.

"Why do you care?"

"Because, jackwagon, I can download it for you. The show must go on."

She studied my face and wiped her nose on the back of her hand.

"It's the James Bond theme song by Instrumental Champions." The black-and-white dance costume made sense, then. It was meant to look like a tuxedo. The dancers even had plastic squirt guns stuck in the inside pocket of their vests.

"Okay. No problem," I told her. She gave me a quick nod before going back to barking at all her fellow dancers. I was in my room, on my computer, and out to the barn in ten minutes flat, a freshly burned CD twirling around my finger.

"Thank you," Imogene whispered after I played the music for her. That was smart. I could've downloaded any ridiculous song and her troupe would've had to improvise. But I was feeling . . . well, I was feeling *nice*, and I had decided not to mess with her. For now..

"You're welcome. Thanks for putting this whole routine together and for helping the abbey and everything." I'd heard she'd been working everyone to the bone for the last couple of weeks and the girls in her advanced jazz class pretty much hated her now, but since it was for a good cause I couldn't help respecting her for it.

"Good luck on your stunt riding, Bernice," Imogene said, and she gave me a smile that almost felt friendly.

• • • •

The metal bleachers filled up by late afternoon. It was almost showtime. I scanned the crowd from behind the barn doors. I didn't know who I was looking for. Maybe one person in the audience who'd root for me? I imagined riding Hoof Hearted out into the pasture to the sound of silence and I shuddered. People better clap, dang it. Whether they like me or not.

Francie stuck her head out the doors just below mine.

"It's getting full out there," she said.

"Yup."

"There's my mom and dad!" She waved furiously at a pair of nice-looking grown-ups. The mom had the same wild red hair as Francie and the dad had her same stubby nose. Together they would look like a family.

I thought about my family. Momma, my lughead brothers, even Lloyd. We'd never been the kind of family to do stuff together or wear white shirts and khaki pants to get our pictures taken on the beach. But I felt a strange twist in my gut when I remembered them. I missed those dingdongs. But at that moment I even missed my moldy old couch, so that's not saying much.

I saw a fat kid with a bowlette and I thought about Chucknorris. Momma always gave him that haircut: she trimmed around a bowl on top and left a long ponytail in the back. I blinked hard to make sure it wasn't my brother. I didn't think anyone else would do that to their head.

"I guess we'd better hide out until the show starts, huh?" Francie grabbed my arm and I was about to pull my head out from between the doors when I stopped dead in my tracks.

From the back row of the bleachers I heard a booming voice say, "I swear, Austin Buttman, if stupid could fly, you'd be a jet!"

I squinted at the rows of people.

"Hey, I kept her between the ditches. You could've driven if you wanted to." I zeroed in on Austin's voice in the crowd and drew in a sharp breath. They were here. They were all here. Momma, Lloyd, Austin, Gordon, Chucknorris, and Busey. They looked uncomfortable with their wide backsides squished on the narrow metal benches, but they'd come!

I dragged Francie out of the barn and weaved through the crowd to find my family. But when I got right up next to them, I didn't know what to say.

"Bernice!" Busey yelled, bolting off the bench and wrapping me in a tight, smelly hug. I mumbled a "Hi" into his shirt and then he passed me down the line. I got squeezed by every one of them before they released me, dazed and sweaty, from the end of the Buttman line. Francie had gotten passed down, too. She looked wide-eyed, but she had a smile on her face like she'd swallowed a coat hanger.

"I didn't know you had so many brothers," she whispered to me.

"Look at you in your cowgirl gear. You look real pretty, little sister," said Austin.

I shrugged, but my face was full of happy.

"Momma, I didn't know you were coming," I said. She had her hair pulled back in a purple scrunchie and I even detected a little bit of makeup.

"Well, I was just gonna come up here to fetch you, but the boys heard about your Action Movie Night and they wanted to come."

"Don't worry," said Busey. "We paid our way, fair and square. Who knew we'd be paying admission to watch our sister ride a horse?"

My cheeks burned, but my head felt like it might float away.

"Do good, little sister," said Busey.

Austin slapped me on the back. "Make us proud."

"Don't break your neck." Chucknorris smiled.

"We'll be the ones yelling our brains out for ya," Gordon said.

The feel-good was filling me up from head to toe. I had a whole cheering section! Francie and I were about to duck back into the barn again when I heard my name.

"Bernice!" The voice was louder than I'd ever heard it before, because any other time I'd heard it was inside a library.

"Ms. Knightley?" The slender librarian waved to me from a few rows up.

I ran to her and Francie followed in my wake.

"What in the blazes are you doing here?" I asked. "Not that I'm not glad to see you!"

"Well, I asked your mother how you were doing when she came into the library last week. She's been applying for jobs using the library's computers. Did you know that?

Anyway, she was bragging about you and how you planned this whole event to help the nuns and I wanted to come see for myself and tell you how proud I am of you."

I wrapped her in a tight hug and I realized we were darn near the same height now. I must have gotten taller!

"Francie, this is Ms. Knightley. She's pretty much the only friend I've ever had."

Francie shook the librarian's hand, but her smile didn't quite touch her eyes.

I yammered on, telling Ms. Knightley all about my routine and introducing her to Mr. Newton, who was in the row in front of her. They talked about me like I wasn't even there, about how smart I was and what a great mind I had. My cheeks blushed hotter than the devil's armpit.

Francie must have slipped back into the barn sometime during that conversation. I guessed she wasn't all that interested in the ghosts of my past.

Then Aunt Josephine stepped up onto the stage and banged the microphone a few times to test if it was working. A round circle of light shined on her from the spotlights that we'd borrowed from the high school. The *Mission: Impossible* theme song started to boom through the speakers and everyone got still and settled.

"Ladies and gentlemen. Your mission, should you choose to accept it, is about to begin."

31

Lights, Camera, Action

Six serious-faced kids filed across the stage, dressed in their white *karategi*. (I'd had to Google what those outfits were called.) They stood on specially marked spots and held their arms stiff at their sides. Their eyes bored holes in the floor until the high-energy pop music started, signaling the Halfway Karate School to start their routine. They sprang into action, striking different fighting poses and yelling together. The audience clapped along to the music and oohed and aahed in all the right places. The performers took turns holding boards up for each other to chop and kick. When Francie successfully broke hers on the first try I hooted and hollered my head off from the crack in the barn doors. She must not have heard me, though, 'cause she didn't look in my direction.

The karate school ended their demonstration by making a sort of human pyramid, with the tiniest fighter straddling the top in a defensive pose. I had an Old Bernice urge to go give the whole bottom row wedgies, but I pushed the thought right out of my head. I was starting to be at least halfway nice. Maybe it was due to living in the town of Halfway. Maybe being here was destined to change me . . . at least half of the way.

The karate kids left the stage to thundering applause, and Imogene's dance troupe quickly found their starting positions. Imogene looked pasty and sweaty, but she plastered on a big fake smile. Once the music started she launched into her James Bond routine without missing a single step. She was a pretty good dancer. I searched the audience from my spot behind the barn doors and saw Mayor Franklin smiling and tapping his foot to the music.

The performance would've been perfect if two of the dancers hadn't accidentally backed into each other with plastic guns drawn. They managed to knock each other off balance and both ended up in a heap. Imogene watched them out of the corner of her eye, her mouth still stretched in that stage smile. The girls hopped back up and found their place in the routine faster than butter melting on a stack of pancakes.

The troupe finished the performance with a bang. For real. The end of the music sounded like a bomb going off and all of them hit the floor and played dead, while the audience went wild. I clapped politely and scanned the crowd for my family once again.

Austin and Gordon talked and laughed, their heads

bent close together. They were annoying enough that the people in front of them asked them to be quiet. My stomach did a little flip-flop seeing my brothers the way the people of Halfway must see them—loud and obnoxious and very Buttman-like.

I watched Chucknorris pull a squishy piece of beef jerky out of his pocket and chew it. He looked bored, and a little rumpled.

Busey made fart noises with his armpits like a champ, and a few of the parents around him glared. My brothers were doofuses but I loved them, even when they were completely embarrassing.

I scanned the audience for Momma.

She was gone. I sucked in a sharp breath. Maybe she had to go take a pee, was all? Maybe she'd be right back. Maybe she was having a cigarette someplace where people wouldn't cough and give her mean looks. But her duct-taped purse wasn't waiting for her on the bleachers.

And that's when I noticed Ms. Knightley was gone, too. Something in my stomach twisted tight.

The Halfway Primary School's archery club took the stage next. Two boys around my age, and one kindergarten-sized girl. They wore Robin Hood costumes, which I don't consider an action movie, but *oh, well.* The girl smiled cutely with her teeny-tiny bow and arrow slung across her back. They'd chosen Renaissance music and had large round targets set up on the right-hand side of the stage.

One by one they fired arrows into the middle of the targets, and the audience erupted in applause. Even the tiny girl got a hole in one, or whatever you call it when you manage to stick your arrow in the middle of the target.

My stomach churned as I thought about Momma and Ms. Knightley taking off in the middle of the performances. All of a sudden my nose couldn't stop itching. Ever since I was a bitty baby an itchy nose meant something bad was gonna happen. I tried to wave to Austin from the crack in the barn doors, but he was still annoying the girl in front of him. I wanted to ask him to go look for Momma and Ms. Knightley. I tried to call to him, softly, but that was when the Renaissance music came to a crashing crescendo.

Onstage, the archery club set up their grand finale, and Robin Hood girl took aim at an apple, which sat on the older boy's head. He wore a blindfold. I was glad she didn't.

The tiny archer drew back her bowstring just as I saw a flash of Momma's purple scrunchie disappearing around the side of the church. I yelled "Momma!" when the girl let her arrow fly, and the crowd let out a noisy gasp.

"Ouch!" yelled the blindfolded kid, and he wiped at his bloody ear while the archer girl glared meaner than a rattlesnake in a frying pan.

"Thanks a lot, Buttman!" she spat. My brothers laughed so hard they sent earthquake tremors through the bleachers. I mouthed to Busey, "Where's Momma?" and he shrugged.

I turned around and found Francie among the performers in the barn. She slumped against the wall, looking sadder than my once-upon-a-time pretend dog Farkle.

"Hey. Why aren't you with your parents? You can go sit by them now."

"You'd love that," she mumbled.

What the what? I didn't have time for Francie's shenanigans. I wanted to find my momma and Ms. Knightley and get ready to ride old Hoof to thundering applause.

"Hey, can you do me a favor?" I asked Francie. Maybe she could run and look for them.

"Why don't you ask the *only* friend you ever had." Francie stood up and stormed out of the barn, leaving me in a puddle of confusion.

Francie was mad at me.

The archery club was pretty mad at me.

And my momma and Ms. Knightley were missing.

I felt lower than a snake's belly in a wagon rut.

• • • •

I paced the dirt floor, bumping into the few performers who were waiting to go on. It was hot in the barn, even though it was cool outside, and it was weirdly quiet for being half full of people in costumes.

I was freaking out.

My insides felt shakier than Momma's washing machine on the spin cycle. I took off my wide-brimmed hat and swiped at my forehead, my toes curling up inside my dirty sneakers. When had everything gone so wrong? One minute you're basking in the excitement of an audience full of friends and family, and the next minute people are disappearing and yelling at you and hating you real good.

I felt a hand on my shoulder and whipped around, hoping it was Momma or Ms. Knightley.

It took me a second to recognize Aunt Josephine because . . . well, she was green. Her face was painted green and she wore a green sweat suit and a green stocking cap instead of her regular habit. Oh, and she had a purple mask tied around her eyes. I blinked a bunch of times.

"Hey, I saw what happened with the archers. You shouldn't worry about it. That boy didn't need the very tip of his ear, anyway." Aunt Josephine gave my shoulder a squeeze and looked closely at my face. "Are you okay, Bernice?"

I let out a shaky breath and tried to fill her in all that had happened. I wanted to cry, to bury my head in Aunt Josephine's squishy (green?) hug and sob like a baby. How had I managed to screw everything up?

"Honey, I'm sure your momma is fine. She probably went to get some popcorn," Aunt Josephine said.

"Or beer," Sister Marie Francis added. She'd appeared

out of nowhere and tilted the brim of my cowgirl hat up so she could see my eyes. She was wearing the green getup, too—red mask, though.

Aunt Josephine glared at her and she shrugged.

"But what about Ms. Knightley? She's not going on a beer run."

"Maybe she got a phone call and didn't want to be rude and answer it during the performance?"

I gave Aunt Josephine a raised-eyebrow look.

"She seems polite enough."

There was a heavy pause, and the oldest of the trio padded over to us calmly, a plastic turtle shell strapped to her thin shoulders. "*Curiouser and curiouser*," said Sister Angela-Clarence. The nuns surrounded me like a sturdy green wall, and I felt my chest unscrew a little bit.

"What's with the outfits?" I asked.

Sister Marie Francis shifted her weight from one foot to the other. "We've been working on a reenactment. We added ourselves to the lineup just before you."

"What kind of reenactment?" I asked, eyes narrowing.

My aunt ducked her head. "We will be re-creating a fight scene from *Teenage Mutant Ninja Turtles*. Some of the other parishioners will pose as bad guys."

I giggled in spite of my nose still itching something fierce.

Aunt Josephine leaned closer. "Maybe we should go look for them?"

I shook my head furiously. "No. I can't go anywhere. I've got to stay here. My performance is the grand finale of the whole show."

Sister Marie Francis glanced at Hoof in his stall, saddled and ready. "Then we'll have to make sure you're back here in time. You can't ride like I know you can if your head is stuffed full of worries. Let's go find them."

"I don't know," I said, biting my bottom lip. Where could they be? Were they together, or did they both decide to leave?

"Maybe a quick look around the grounds and the church?" Sister Marie Francis asked.

I let out a gush of hot air. "Okay. But we have to be back here in fifteen minutes. Tops. The show must go on."

The nuns nodded and led me out of the dimly lit barn into the sunshine of the spring day. I felt a bubble of hope that we'd find Momma and Ms. Knightley, but at the same time I felt that familiar dread. Something bad was gonna happen. I scratched at my itchy, traitorous nose.

• • • •

The nuns and I hurried to the church and checked all the bathrooms, looking for Momma and Ms. Knightley. I could hear cannons firing every once in a while and wondered if it was the Halfway Historical Society doing their Civil War reenactment, or if the Future Circus Performers of

Halfway had shot someone out of a cannon. I wished I'd paid closer attention to the lineup.

The three of us checked the downstairs living area and the grounds all around the building without a sign of the missing audience members. It was bright out, with wispy white clouds hanging low in the sky. I scanned the trees lining the pasture for the glow of a cigarette or a moving shadow. Everything was still and quiet. Except for the occasional cannon blast.

"They've disappeared. Gone." Aunt Josephine folded her arms across her chest.

I frowned, thinking like a brainiac. *Where could they be? Where haven't we looked?* "Wait. Did any of us check inside the sanctuary?"

The three nuns in their ninja turtle outfits looked at each other and shrugged. "The sanctuary is locked. That's where we put all the money from the ticket sales." A look of understanding passed over my aunt's face, and she and I sprinted to the wide porch.

"If anyone could break into a locked church . . . ," I said under my breath.

She did the sign of the cross while she ran. "God help that girl."

Sure enough, the large double doors of the sanctuary were closed, but somehow no longer locked. We busted in there, blinking in the dim light, and stood frozen at the scene.

Momma was gripping the green metal cash box. Ms. Knightley was trying with all her skinny librarian strength to pry the box out of Momma's hands.

"What in the devil?" Aunt Josephine's wide eyes scanned the floor, taking in the scattered five-dollar bills and the two women tug-of-warring right in front of the Jesus-on-the-cross. Neither one of them seemed to notice us standing openmouthed in the doorway.

"Let go, you witch!" But as much as Momma squirmed, her tiny opponent held on tight.

Ms. Knightley yanked the cash box again. "I will not let you destroy everything your daughter has worked so hard for. That money belongs to the abbey!"

Momma jerked the box back toward her, sweat beading on her forehead. I don't think I'd ever seen her put so much effort into anything. "I need it more than them nuns do. I got bills to pay and children to feed, and my boyfriend and I need to get back to California for some more auditions."

Thoughts swirled around my head like smoke. She was trying to steal the same money I'd thought about stealing not too many months ago. I remembered the temptation, like a strong magnet, trying to pull me to the dark side. But then I'd talked to Aunt Josephine, and I'd decided I wanted to help her instead of steal from her. Momma couldn't muster up the same decency for her own sister. My mouth went sour, like I'd just bit a lemon, and I wanted to punch her in her selfish guts.

"Ladies! This is no way to behave in the house of the Lord!" Aunt Josephine bellowed in her best nun voice.

The women froze, finally realizing they weren't alone.

"I can explain," Momma said at the exact same time Ms. Knightley released the cash box and pointed a shaking finger.

"She was trying to take your money!"

"Josephine, I wasn't gonna steal this. You know that. What happened, you see, is I prayed for this money. This exact amount. And the Lord told me to come in here and get it. I was supposed to use it for my purposes, and then God was gonna give me more to replace it."

Ms. Knightley was breathing hard. "Did the Lord tell you to use your credit card to break into the locked church?" I'd never seen her look so fuming mad.

Aunt Josephine walked over to her sister and took the cash box from her sweaty hand. "The Lord didn't let me in on His plans. And until He does, this money belongs to St. Drogo's, to use however we deem fit."

I felt a tweak of guilt somewhere in a dusty corner of my heart, because, after all, I was still hoping to somehow get my hands on some of the *leftover* money to pay for stunt camp. But that was not the same as plain old stealing it. Me and Momma were not the same. I was at least halfway honest.

"I can't believe this. Even from you, Momma. Stealing right under the nose of the Lord Jesus. It's downright shady." I looked her straight in the eye and my voice didn't wobble one little bit.

She scowled and squinted at the box, her forehead shiny with effort. "Don't go getting all preachy on me, Bernice. Only reason you're here is 'cause you scammed a whole mess of people out of their cash."

Ms. Knightley turned to look at me, but I couldn't quite meet her eye.

"That's right, book lady. My daughter ran an illegal fund-raising hoax straight out of your precious library."

My cheeks flamed, and I didn't dare glance at Ms. Knightley, but then she surprised me by coming right up to me and taking my hand. "It's okay, Bernice. Whatever you did before, I'm sure you're sorry. And if I know one thing about Bernice Buttman, it's that she learns from her mistakes."

My aunt nodded her agreement, and I felt my shoulders relax a fraction of an inch.

Momma changed tactics. "Sweetheart, I am so, so proud of all you've done here. Helping my sourpuss sister and her habit-wearing buddies. It's real nice. But aren't you about ready to come home?"

A million pictures exploded in my brain at that word.

A moldy couch.

A horse pasture.

A flattened trampoline.

A burning pencil.

A living room full of motorcycle parts.

A circle of green sweat suits.

A smelly headlock.

A red-penciled A on my homework.

A curly-haired boy's nose, dangerously close to doggy doo.

A redheaded girl who used to be my first-ever friend.

"I think . . ." My voice squeaked a little bit. "I think Halfway has become my home."

Aunt Josephine pulled me into a squishy hug, and I was surrounded by the smell of her laundry soap and lavender hand lotion. "You can stay here for as long as you want, Bernice."

Ms. Knightley straightened her disheveled clothes and smiled firmly at me. "You're different here, Bernice. And I think it's good."

I hugged her back. Even though she's as skinny as a spaghetti noodle, she squeezed me real tight, pressing my cheek to her sharp collarbone. Two hugs in under two minutes. *Guess I've gone soft.*

Momma's face looked slack and defeated in the pale light of the stained glass. She pulled her ponytail tighter, her lips pressed in a thin white line.

"Don't we still have a riding demonstration to watch?" Ms. Knightley asked me. She plucked my cowgirl hat off the ground, where all the huggin' had knocked it, and plopped it on my head.

I smiled so hard my cheeks hurt, then said a silent prayer of thanks to St. Drogo, the patron saint of ugly people, 'cause he'd really come through for me this time.

32

Sealed with a Booger

When I got back to the barn, there were fewer performers roaming around, because most of the acts had already gone. I could hear the Halfway Junior High School's choir singing a rousing rendition of "Eye of the Tiger," from the *Rocky* movies.

> *Rising up, back on the street*
> *Did my time, took my chances . . .*

There was one more chance *I* needed to take before me and Hoof entered the arena. He stomped at me, but I headed in the direction of the girl hugging her knees against the barn wall. Francie.

She didn't look up when I stopped in front of her, even though I blocked the light like a giant Bernice-shaped eclipse. I shifted nervously from sneaker to sneaker and then cleared my throat loudly.

"Ahem."

She looked right through me.

I could still hear the junior high choir, and their voices gave me courage, so I straightened up and stomped my shoe.

"Hey. I'm new at this friendship thing, and so if you're mad at me or somethin' you better tell me what I did so I can apologize and we can both move on with our lives."

"Why don't you ask your librarian? Your *only* friend in the world, wasn't that what you called her?"

It finally dawned on me why Francie was sore. She was *jealous* of Ms. Knightley. I snort-laughed and slapped my knee.

"Ms. Knightley is a *grown-up*! She can't be my best friend. She was the only person who was nice to me up in Kansas City, but you know, it's not the same as having a friend my own age."

"Did you say *best* friend?" Francie wiped her nose on the sleeve of her white robe.

"Best and only." I smiled my dimpliest grin at her, and Francie smiled back at me.

"And here's something else. I'm gonna stay in Halfway for a while. At least until the end of the school year. I think I fit here, ya know?"

"I think you fit here just great."

The choir sang about their fights of glory and dreams of the past. My dreams for the future included a brand-new best friend, and I felt like making it official.

"Hey. I got an idea. We should be booger sisters."

She smirked. "Don't you mean blood sisters?"

"I did some Googling, and it turns out there are a lot of blood-borne diseases. But I have yet to find any booger-borne ones."

Francie swallowed hard, but she stood up and dug her index finger deep into her nostril, as I did the same. Then, when we'd both got a good one, we smooshed them together.

"Friends?" I said.

"Friends."

We wiped our fingers on our shirts and hugged real quick.

"Wish me luck," I said, as the final notes of "Eye of the Tiger" faded into the thundering applause from the audience. I punched the air a few times, Rocky-style, and Francie did, too.

"Oh my gosh! I almost forgot! I got you something. For good luck." She felt around in the shadows near where she'd been sitting and pulled out a big, lidded box.

"What is it?" I asked, instantly suspicious. You can take the bully out of the girl, but she'll probably slug you in the arm and take it back. Old habits die hard, and all that.

"It's a present." She rolled her eyes. "Open it."

I pushed the lid off the box and waited for the paper snakes to hit me in the face. Instead I was hit in the face with the smell of leather.

"Boots," I breathed, taking one of the soft brown cowgirl boots out of the paper folded around them.

"My aunt Edna gets me a pair every year, and I am *so not* a cowgirl. I thought they'd work better than those horrible sneakers you always wear." She wrinkled her nose as I took off my shoes and slid my socked foot into the new boots.

"Well, butter my butt and call me a biscuit," I muttered. "I did not make a mistake when I picked you for my only friend."

"Best friend," Francie corrected, and we both mimed picking our noses and wiping the boogers on our shirts. It would be our secret handshake from now on. Booger sisters for life.

I tipped my hat at her and then led Hoof Hearted through his gate and toward our destiny.

• • • •

Hoof's neck trembled beneath my hand as I led him out into the arena. The audience members sat on the edge of their benches, leaning toward the wooden fence to watch the Action Movie Night's grand finale. That was me and Hoof. And we were ready. Except both of us wanted to pee our pants, and horses don't even wear pants.

My brothers lined up against the north side of the fence, a solid wall of cut-off T-shirts and ripped-up jeans. They hollered as soon as we took our places in the middle of the arena.

"Go, little sister!"

"Show us what you got!"

"Yee-haw, cowgirl!"

"Don't crack your skull!"

I waved limply in their direction, but my thin smile didn't make it to my brain. I was going over each and every move of my routine in my head and trying not to think about what would happen if I screwed it all up. I kinda wondered about Momma and Ms. Knightley, but I spotted them next to my brothers. Momma gave me a soft smile and a nod. Ms. Knightley clapped enthusiastically and stuck her pinky fingers in her mouth and let out a sharp whistle.

Hoof and I waited awkwardly for the music to start. I picked a wedgie and tried to mentally prepare myself. My hands shook and my pits were sweaty.

I spotted the nuns, still dressed in their ninja turtle outfits. Their "totally rad" routine would have the people of Halfway's jaws flapping for years to come. Who knew that Aunt Josephine could kick her leg so high?

With the words to "Eye of the Tiger" still running through my head, I stared down at my new boots and let out a slow breath.

"This is it, Hoof. Time to show Halfway what we're made of."

I stood beside him, loosely holding the reins, and when

the music blared we started walking. I did my one, two, three hops with my legs together and then sprang one leg clean over Hoof's back. I was on board, and the crowd went wild. I finally smiled and led him into a fast gallop around the pasture a few times before attempting my next trick.

I waited until I was right in front of my family and the chorus blared, and then I slowed Hoof to a canter and in one smooth motion swung around backward in the saddle. I did a full lap with the reins behind me, the rhythm of the canter all backward, but I managed to not fall off, and the audience paid me in applause. So far, so good. One last trick to get through and I'd be home free.

I flipped frontways, which was still a trick when Hoof was hoofin' it, and got ready for our grand finale. I couldn't spare a look at my family, but I pictured them watching me with jaws dragging on the floor. Who knew Bernice Buttman could be good at anything?

At exactly the right time in my music, I raced Hoof across the middle of the pasture and let him smooth out his gait. I swung my boots up on the saddle and stood, the slick soles barely giving me enough traction. I held the reins loosely in my hands, and my knees bent and bobbed in time to Hoof's stride. The wind tugged at my hat and made my cheeks pink, but the sounds of cheering from the crowd kept me glued to the saddle.

When we'd done a whole lap around the pasture, I sat

down and waved at all my fans. It reminded me of when they crowned the Lone Star Trailer Park Queen every year and pulled her royal wagon behind a four-wheeler. Only, people looked much happier to see me than Sue Ellen Fester, because she seemed to win the title every dang year. We all thought she rigged it.

Hoof and me came right up to where my family watched. His backside jerked toward the fence and then came to a complete stop, sending me flying sideways toward the dirt. At least, I wished it was dirt.

The crowd was quiet for a second, until I waved my hat in the air, letting them know I was all right. My ears rang with the sounds of all those people clapping and cheering for me. Or maybe the ringing was from my brains getting a little rattled on the dismount.

Before I'd even stood up to take my bow, I was surrounded by people who loved me. The nuns squished me in a masked green hug. My brothers took turns trying to stuff my head into their armpits. Francie wiped a booger on my shirt, but in the nicest possible way. Ms. Knightley held my shoulders out at arm's length and told me how proud she was of me. Hoof nuzzled me with his nose, asking for forgiveness for his little bit of improvisation there at the end. I gave him a tight hug around the neck and slipped him a sugar cube.

Momma didn't make a big fuss, but I saw her swipe at

tears leaking out of her eyes. She squeezed my hand and I squeezed back.

I led the crowd over to the bleachers as the sun started to slip behind the barn. We settled in with buttery tubs of popcorn and watched Wonder Woman save the day. As I sat squished on the bench between Francie and Ms. Knightley, my heart felt like it might just swell to bursting.

33

Pot Lucky

The nuns wouldn't tell me how much money we'd raised on Action Movie Night. They wanted to announce it to everyone at St. Drogo's at the same time, so after service on the very next Sunday we organized a potluck lunch as a kind of celebration.

If you've never been to a church potluck, you're missing out. Even though St. Drogo's only had twelve patrons, everybody and their uncle shows up when food's involved. And they brought all the good stuff. I filled my plate with fried chicken, biscuits, Jell-O salad, potato salad, cheesy grits, and three kinds of desserts. Then my plate ripped in half on my way back to my table and my lunch went all over the floor and down the front of my D.A.R.E T-shirt, so I had to go all through the line again.

Momma and my brothers had left right after *Wonder Woman*, but not without giving me one last squeeze. Momma promised to write to me, and to look into some acting jobs right here in Missouri. My brothers said they missed me, but Austin mentioned he'd been sleeping on my couch, and I shuddered to think about how it must smell covered in his BO and morning breath. Momma had agreed to let me stay with Aunt Josephine until the end of the summer, and then we would decide about my sixth-grade year.

Francie had gotten the Principal's Citizenship Award. Yup, my do-gooder best friend had managed to be more of a global citizen than even Imogene. Francie wore the little plastic pin they'd given her ever since the big announcement and school-wide assembly, but whenever I said anything to her about it, she just blushed as red as a tomato and said it was nothing. Imogene never said a word about the award, not even to congratulate Francie, but I'd run into her a few times at the Halfway Paradise Retirement Village. Seemed that both of us didn't mind helping our communities, even when nobody was watching.

Father Wilson said grace to thank God for our food, and I was glad he did because I was feeling pretty thankful in my own heart. I had a friend. I was getting good grades in school. And I had a home here in Halfway. I quietly told God thanks before I added my amen to the chorus and did the sign of the cross for good measure.

Sister Mary Margaret (my aunt Josephine) stood up at the head of the table after Father Wilson was done, and all eyes fixed on her.

"As you know, our congregation has been struggling to raise the funds necessary to pay our debts and keep our doors open." Suspense hung in the air as thick as Sister Marie Francis's morning oatmeal.

"With the money raised at last week's Action Movie Night, put together by my own niece, Bernice"—she gestured to me—"we have more than enough to keep St. Drogo's afloat."

The congregation broke into applause, and I looked around from happy face to happy face.

"I've talked to her mother, trying to get ideas for how we could show Bernice how much we appreciate all the work she did for us." I felt my heart catch in my throat.

"As a token of our gratitude, we would like to send Bernice to the summer camp of her choice." She looked at me and smiled. "Anywhere you want, Bernice."

Hollywood Hills Stunt Camp.

All I'd wanted for the last year was to get away from the Lone Star Trailer Park and to find a place where I belonged. Where I was good at something. Where I could make friends.

Hollywood Hills Stunt Camp was 1,624.6 miles away from the Loser Trailer Park.

But a few too many miles away from Halfway.

Learning to punch people harder wasn't as appealing anymore.

As I looked around the crowded church, at all those

hopeful faces, my lungs blew up like a hunk of Hubba Bubba. Everyone was smiling for me. Everyone was clapping for me. I fit in here like a square peg in a square hole, and I'd never been so happy to be a square.

And then I remembered the feeling I'd had when I'd stood on Hoof's back and the crowd roared. I was already good at something. Really good.

I stood up, almost tipping over my bottle of Mountain Dew, but luckily Sister Marie Francis caught it in her rough hand. "If you don't mind, I think I'd like to stay here and keep taking riding lessons with Sister Marie Francis and Hoof Hearted."

The congregation clapped politely, and Sister Marie Francis wrapped me in a wild and crazy hug that sent my Mountain Dew flying to the floor.

And one by one, the ugly folks (which St. Drogo's was the patron saint of) came by and shook my hand and told me how glad they were I'd come to their town. They looked different now, in the soft light of the stained-glass sanctuary, and I thought to myself how funny it was that people got better-looking when they shook your hand and told you how much they liked you. Maybe even Bernice Buttman was beautiful, if you gave her the chance to prove it.

Acknowledgments

Seeing this little story that I wrote for myself become a real live book has been one of the greatest joys of my life. I have so very many people to thank for helping that dream become a reality!

First of all, I would like to give a shout-out to my agent, Kate Testerman. Thank you for being my very first "yes."

To Caroline Abbey at Random House, thank you for helping me find the very best version of this story, and for helping me cut down on the number of fart jokes.

To Linzie Hunter and Isabel Warren-Lynch for making all my cover dreams come true!

To my fabulous copyeditors, Barbara Bakowski and Barbara Perris . . . I am sorry. I have no idea where commas go. Thank you for helping me seem like I know what I'm doing.

To the Woodneath Writers Group, Novel Nineteens, the Pitch Wars family, the Twitter writing community, and the Querying Authors Facebook page, thank you all for being so encouraging and helpful.

Thank you to Michelle Merrill, Nancy Banks, Kristin Van Risseghem, Kari Mahara, Shelly Steig, Katherine Settle, Polly McCann, and Carrie Allen for reading early and late drafts of this book and lending me your eyeballs and your brains.

To the people of Halfway, Missouri, thank you for letting me take some liberties with your town. I just really wanted Bernice to go live somewhere with nice people and a fun name.

To my closest friends and family, thank you for not laughing in my face when I said I was going to be an author. That was cool of you. I love you all.

To Carrie Chambers, middle-grade teacher extraordinaire, thank you for letting me use your students as guinea pigs and for always being my biggest fan.

To my Jennie, the best critique partner and friend a girl could have. It was fate that brought us together at that first writers' group meeting on a snowy January night! You have inspired me to keep going these last several years, and I have loved learning and growing with you on this madcap adventure. Thank you for always celebrating with me and for reading my truly terrible first drafts.

To Caleb, Loralie, and Roman, I love you more than life. And more than cheese balls.

Dad + Grace = the perfect team

So what happens when Dad tries to add someone new to the team?

Operation: Stepmom Shake-Up

Read on for a sneak peek!

Bea arrived right on time hauling a stack of teen magazines and a giant bag of Skittles. She bounced into the living room and plopped on the couch where I was "resting." Actually, I was pouting, but Dad didn't seem to be catching on.

"Hayley Mills or Lindsay Lohan?" she asked, kicking her sneakers up on the coffee table.

"Huh?"

"I thought we wanted to watch *The Parent Trap* for prank-spiration while your dad is on his date?"

"Oh. Right. I don't care—pick whatever you want." I knew my mind wouldn't be able to focus on anything other than my dad breaking up Team Gravy.

Dad sprinted downstairs wearing clean jeans and a button-down shirt. He had gel in his hair and he'd shaved, and it wasn't even Sunday.

"Well, girls, I hope I can trust you to stay out of trouble.

I'll be home early. Like by ten. Everything in Springdale is closed by ten, isn't it?"

The two of us are pretty much never out late on a Saturday night, so I had no answer for him.

"We'll be fine, Pastor Davy," Bea said.

"Have fun with the woman you hit on at the grocery store." I crossed my arms over my chest.

"What?" Dad spurted.

"Oh, sorry. Did she hit on you first?"

Bea's eyebrows shot up, and she watched us go back and forth like she was watching a tennis match. I was pretty sure she'd never witnessed me and my dad fight in the whole six years she'd been my friend.

"Nobody 'hit on' anybody, Grace. Geez, how do you even know that expression?"

I rolled my eyes.

"Will you two be all right here?" He stuck his chin out at me, daring me to tell him to stay home. I wanted to. I wanted to so very, very badly. There was no way Rachel-from-the-grocery-store could ever make us as happy as my mom had. My mind searched frantically for some stick of dynamite to throw at this situation, but I was coming up blank.

"Fine. Go on your ridiculous date. I hope you have a wonderful time and fly to Vegas to get married."

"Grace . . ."

I buried my face in a pillow while Bea walked him to the door. Dad pulled a crisp twenty out of his wallet and handed it to Bea for the pizza delivery. It was just the inspiration I needed.

I hopped up and gave my dad a quick and furious hug. It took him a second or so, but then he squeezed me back hard. He was so distracted by my light-speed mood change he didn't notice when I snuck his wallet out of his back pocket. He turned toward the door, and I tossed my prize on the couch before giving Dad one last wave.

And then he was gone, and my half of Team Gravy curdled.

"So I guess our plan was a dud?" Bea grabbed the remote from the table.

I smiled. "Operation: Stepmom Shake-Up is in full effect. Although somewhat delayed and not very well thought out."

Bea scratched her head. "Huh?"

I snatched up the wallet I'd tossed on the couch and waved it at her.

"I snagged this. Guess dinner is on Rachel." I chuckled at my own genius.

Bea shook her head as she ate a handful of purple and yellow Skittles. "That wasn't on the list."

I shrugged. "Sometimes you have to improvise."

While we watched the clueless twins prank each other

at camp, I told Bea about my failure to fake the flu in the bookstore.

Bea scratched Potus behind the ear. "But, you know, you could get a stepmom out of this whole thing. That could be kinda . . . nice."

"Stepmoms are never nice. Take the Cinderella story, for example. Plus, me and Dad have worked overtime to stay afloat after the accident. We don't need anyone messing up our system."